A BABY FOR THE COWBOY

LINDA GOODNIGHT

1

Levi Donley had never felt more alone. Surrounded by people beneath a sodden sky, he wished he was anywhere on earth but here in Calypso, Oklahoma.

His brother was dead. All because of Choctaw Creek, a stream that flowed right through the center of town, calm and harmless. Most of the time.

Yet every few years, spring rains brought deluges, and water fell in sheets to fill the creek and swamp streets. Flash floods. Dangerous. Deadly.

Everybody in the whole county knew about Choctaw Creek. The trouble was, most never believed the flooding would be quite as bad as it was. During every downpour, impatient Okies braved the standing water, confident their vehicles, particularly the pickup trucks, could ford the stream unharmed.

But not everyone made it.

And the results were tragic.

Levi shifted from his bad leg to his worse leg, Stetson crushed tight against a chest threatening to explode with grief. Scott. His only sibling. Swept away by the current. Lost. Drowned. Along with the wife Levi hadn't known existed.

He still couldn't believe the news. His brain simply would not make the connection. Scott was strong and smart, a rancher who understood the whims of nature. How could this have happened to him?

Levi closed his eyes for a moment. When he opened them, he was still here, in Calypso Cemetery. He stood a few feet from the green awning that sheltered funeral attendees he should recognize but didn't quite. He'd been gone too long. Better to stay out of the way. Talking might cause a firestorm of sorrow to spew forth and embarrass them all.

The preacher, a bright-faced brick of a man somewhere around Levi's age of thirty-two, read the Twenty-Third psalm. Levi had a vague memory of learning the Scripture as a kid in Vacation Bible School. Thanks to Great Aunt Ruby, he and Scott had attended VBS and every other summer activity in town. He never minded. Anything to escape their dad for a few hours.

As the preacher bowed his head to pray, Levi shifted back to his bad leg. The worse leg was screaming loud enough to make him cry.

He hadn't seen Aunt Ruby in years. Was she still alive?

Or was she, like Scott, gone forever? Another regret he'd have to live with?

The service ended, so the mourners—and there were many in this small town—wandered off to their cars, feet squishing on the still moist earth of Calypso Cemetery. Levi stayed behind to watch as his brother and sister-in-law were lowered into the yawning wet earth. Both of them. Gone.

To make him feel worse, he'd arrived late, missing the church service because his truck broke down on the long drive from Tucson. He'd been stuck somewhere outside of Odessa without a mechanic or a parts store anywhere for miles.

Flying would have been faster, but there was the matter of his horse, his truck, and his trailer. And there was the stronger fact that he'd rather be stomped by a bull than risk his life in an airplane.

Today, he regretted this particular phobia, which was more stubbornness than fear. He could have left the horse and truck in Tucson with a buddy and returned for them after the services. But he'd never expected the alternator to go bad in a two-year-old truck. Nor to be stuck on the flats of Texas waiting for the part to arrive from Dallas.

He clutched the crown of his hat. The felt gave beneath the pressure.

Levi wasn't the crying sort, but as his brother's bronze casket disappeared behind the mound of Oklahoma red dirt, his eyes burned so badly he slid on a pair of sunglasses he'd picked up at a truck stop near Las Cruces. The tears were stuck down there, choking him. He wouldn't let them have their way. He was a man, a cowboy, tough as bull hide.

Scott. Oh, Scott. I should have been here. I should have called you. I should have...

Everything inside him threatened to seize up, a volcano of remorse and anguish.

Fighting the panic, Levi panned the cemetery for a distraction. His gaze stuttered to a halt at the sight of an older couple in conversation with a familiar woman. Black hair. Same size. Couldn't be Emily though. This woman's hair was short, full, behind-the-ears professional. Emily had favored long, straight hair that accented her pale skin and olive cat-eyes. Still, something in the way the woman moved her hands when she talked reminded him of that one time long ago when he might have chosen a different path.

Regrets stung. Every last one of them. And he had plenty.

He watched as the woman with the shining black hair squeezed the older man's arm before walking, head down, toward the parked cars. Her spiky heels stabbed divots into the wet ground.

A strange yearning swirled with the grief.

She wasn't Emily. Couldn't be. Emily wouldn't come near anyone named Donley, even for a funeral.

A hand clapped him on the shoulder and jolted him back into focus as the preacher stepped around to face him. The man was shorter than Levi, but not by much, and stockier. Beneath neatly combed brown hair, he wore a suit, but that's where the preacher stereotype ended. Like rodeo preachers Levi knew, this man was fit, muscled and looked as if he could handle a hammer or a tractor better than a pulpit. The suit coat stretched tight across his broad shoulders.

"You must be Levi."

Levi swallowed, gulped past the sob that hung in his throat like a chicken bone. "Yes, sir."

"I'm Marcus Snider, pastor of Evangel Church. Scott spoke highly of you."

A simple phrase meant to make him feel better had the opposite effect. Levi wanted to yell and beat his head against a gravestone. "We hadn't talked in a while."

He wasn't sure why he'd shared that bit of information, but he hadn't even known about his brother's marriage. What kind of brother didn't know something that important?

He and Scott weren't estranged. Nobody was mad. They'd just drifted apart. Rather, *he* had drifted, far from the little town and the ranch where they'd both been raised. Scott was the brave one. He'd stayed. When Dad passed on three years ago, Levi had come home for exactly one day to pay his last respects. Mostly, he'd come to be sure the old man was really dead. Let Scott have the ranch. He wanted the free life, ranches, rodeos, anywhere but here.

"If there's anything I can do for you, give me a call." The pastor looked too young to do much consoling but the compassion in his eyes and voice was enough for today.

"Appreciate it."

"Scott and Jessica attended my church." The preacher handed him a business card, eyes moist as he cleared his throat. "We're here for you. Anything at all. Scott was a deacon, a real pillar of Evangel Church. He'll be sorely missed."

A deacon? Scott? When had his brother gotten religion? Not that Levi was complaining. Just surprised. His brother was in heaven, where everyone wanted to go. At least, he did. Some far and distant day.

On a deep level, Levi believed that Jesus was the way. He simply wasn't ready to saddle up and ride in that direction. Not yet. Not for a long time. Ranch and rodeo life was rough and hard, and the Christians took a lot of flack. He admired their tenacity, even listened in the arena to Cowboy Church a few Sunday mornings. Otherwise, faith was low on his list. Someday. Maybe. When he was old.

Levi shot a quick glance toward his brother's casket. Scott's road to heaven hadn't been long enough. Not even close. Time was shorter than either of them thought.

With a nod, throat too thick to speak, he took the preacher's card and slid it into the pocket of his western cut sport jacket. Along with crumbling horse cubes, he felt the paper handout from the last funeral he'd attended. A cowboy. Gored by a practice bull. Josh had been a Christian, too. Crosses on his chaps, a Bible on his dashboard, the whole enchilada.

So much death and misery. How could God let that happen to His own followers?

Levi's fingers played with the crumbs as he glanced toward the shade tree where he'd parked his trailer. He needed to get out of here. Away from this cemetery. Out of Calypso. He couldn't take much more, and poor old Freckles had probably had all of that trailer he wanted. Even now, the appaloosa moved restlessly, his hooves echoing against metal.

"Thanks for the service." He was trying to think of

other niceties, but nothing came. Truth was, his mind was a flea circus. He couldn't stay focused on anything very long. If he did, he'd have to remember his little brother was dead, and that hurt too much.

"I suppose you'll be taking over the ranch now." The minister's statement was more of a question.

No chance of that whatsoever. "I haven't had time to think about it."

"I understand. You'll be staying, though, won't you? To settle things and make arrangements."

"I suppose for a day or two." He'd not given that much thought either, but he was the sole heir to the ranch and whatever else Scott had left behind. As much as staying in Calypso very long chafed at him, he supposed he'd have to stick around for a few days. Get Scott's business in order. Sell the ranch. Hightail it for Amarillo.

His attention drifted toward the movement of mourners.

Car doors slammed. Motors revved up. The vehicles lined along the edge of the cemetery began their slow departure. The black-haired woman was nowhere to be seen, and Levi suffered a puzzling quiver of disappointment.

On a nearby grave, an American flag fluttered in the crisp spring breeze. A veteran, he assumed. Overhead, bruised clouds, heavy with impending rain, hovered beneath momentary glimpses of pale blue sky, a fitting mood for a funeral.

His mind was wandering again. He brought his attention back to the preacher. The fresh-faced minister stood close as if he had something to say and wasn't sure where to begin. Levi understood. No amount of preacher platitudes would bring back his brother.

He didn't want to be rude, but he had to get out of here before he exploded.

"Thanks for everything, pastor," he said again, letting the man know he was about to leave.

"One minute, please, Levi." Pastor Snider put a hand on his arm. "You said you hadn't talked to Scott in a while."

"That's right."

"How long?"

Levi pinched his top lip and squinted over the rows and rows of tombstones, ashamed to admit the truth. "Three years maybe." At Dad's funeral?

"And you arrived only this morning?"

The line of questions was starting to wear thin. If the man had something to say, Levi wished he would spit it out. "Yes, sir. About twenty minutes ago. Had some truck trouble on the drive."

"Then you don't know."

He knew way too much. Scott was dead. So was his wife. Flash floods can kill. Anything else didn't matter. "Know what?"

"About Mason, the baby."

Levi got a strange ringing in his ears. "The what? What did you say?"

"Scott and Jessica's baby, Mason. Your nephew survived."

EMILY CALDWELL RESTED her forehead on the steering

wheel of her Nissan Rogue. Jessica hadn't gotten to see the shiny new SUV. She would have giggled at the bold monarch orange and declared it perfect. Jessica loved rich colors.

Emily flipped down the visor mirror to wipe mascara from beneath her eyes and regain some kind of professional demeanor for the conversation she could not avoid.

Levi.

She'd observed him standing alone a short distance from the grave just as she'd watched his truck and trailer rumble down the quiet lane leading from the highway into Calypso Cemetery. He'd been late and had parked beneath a tree away from the other cars.

She had to talk to him whether she wanted to or not. For Jessica. For baby Mason. It was her job. And she had to do it before he disappeared again.

With a deep, shaky breath, she started the Rogue and slowly drove around the cemetery to park next to Levi's silver truck and wait.

From her vantage point, she could see him talking to Pastor Marcus, though he probably couldn't see her. That was for the best. He looked beaten down, as if the years hadn't treated him as well as he'd expected. Grief could do that too, as she could well attest.

A tinge of pity intermingled with the dread of talking to the rangy cowboy. He and Scott had once been inseparable. If he was still the Levi she'd known, he was dying inside. But he'd pretend he wasn't. Cowboy tough, all the way. Though she understood better than most the reasons he hid behind that particular wall.

Reluctant to return to those awful days, even in memory, she got out of the car and went to the trailer. The horse's head, dark chestnut except for the white spots on his muzzle, protruded from the sliding window. At the sight of her, the appaloosa whinnied a soft greeting.

"Hi, there." She raised a palm for him to smell. Warm, moist breath grazed her skin. "You're a good boy. Or girl. No insult intended."

She chuckled a little at the silliness. Naturally, the horse was friendly. Levi had always been best friends with an equine.

Emily stepped up on the bumper and peered inside the trailer. The horsey smell had her leaning back.

"You're probably ready to get out of there, aren't you?"

"Didn't anyone ever tell you not to mess with a man's horse?"

Emily spun, hopping to the ground, her pulse in overdrive. "Levi!"

He dipped his chin. "Emily."

His eyes were so sad she almost put her arms around him. Almost.

"I'm heartsick over Scott and Jessica. I'm so sorry. I can't imagine what you're feeling."

"No. You can't." He shifted to one side as if he were in pain. "What do you want?"

She glanced at his leg and back up again. "We have to talk."

He shook his head, opened the cab door, and slid inside. "Not here. Not now."

"I realize the timing is awful but—"

"Water under the bridge, Em." He slammed the door and cranked the engine.

Standing her ground, she rapped on the window. "Levi, please."

With a less than pleasant expression, he rolled down the window and stared at her without a word. He was hurting, devastated. He wanted to escape. As always, he wanted to run, and like before, he had good reason.

She resisted the increasing urge to soothe him with a touch. "I'm really sorry to bother you, but this is important. Give me a few minutes. Please. That's all I need."

"If it's that important, I'll be at the ranch. But don't expect me to answer the door."

Before she could stop him, he put the truck in gear and left her standing alone.

Again.

But this time she couldn't let him.

2

L evi's F-150 bumped down gravel roads, rattled the two-horse trailer, and caused the patient appaloosa to suck his hooves deeper into the wood floor. Normally attuned to his horse, Levi was far too numb to do more than notice. He was too lost, his insides a gaping, aching hole.

Scott left behind a baby. *A baby.*

No wonder he couldn't think straight.

As he drew closer to the small ranch sprawled across two hundred acres of Bermuda grass and pecan trees, anxiety tightened his shoulders. He considered a quick U-turn and a fast ride to anywhere else.

"Let someone else—*anyone* else—take this place and its rotten memories." The only thing that had ever mattered on this ranch was gone. Six feet under.

All he needed from this place was a good spot to stick a *for sale* sign.

He pulled to a halt next to the front porch, killed the engine, and folded his arms on the steering wheel to stare morosely at his childhood home. A single-story garage protruded from one end of the boxy two-story now painted snow white, a far cry from the ugly brown he remembered.

"Big improvement, Scott," he mumbled. Erase that sorry color and the memory that went with it. Though it wasn't the color that had sent Levi packing. Or even the long, miserable days by himself in the heat with a paint brush and the sound of his father's voice berating him for some infraction. Scott had snuck him cold water when the old man wasn't looking.

The grief hit him again, a massive ocean wave of loss. Rather than bawl like a baby, he got out of the truck and went to the trailer.

Freckles greeted him with a whicker.

Levi pushed open the latches and slung wide the door. The metallic bang reverberated over the silent fields. Freckles' hooves added their rhythm as the appaloosa stepped to the ground. He gave his master a quizzical brown eye before ducking his head to nibble on spring green grass.

The rain that had killed Scott gave life to the grass. Didn't make sense. But then nothing did today; maybe nothing ever had. Not here anyway.

Levi rubbed a hand over the horse's warm neck, emotion boiling and rolling inside. He was so tightly wound he didn't know how to let go. Scott was gone. Levi's only brother. The strong and gentle Donley kid who'd fought with his brain and his smile instead of his fists. Gone. He'd left a son, a baby Levi hadn't known existed.

He had a nephew, a tiny version of his brother.

"Mason." The back of his eyes stung. He was a worthless excuse for a brother. Worthless like the old man said. All those years ago, he'd left Scott to fend for himself, and now his brother was dead and his little boy orphaned.

Everything in Levi wanted to climb back in the truck and drive away from this ranch and Calypso. To run far and fast and never look back again.

But he owed Scott. Even if that meant sticking around the Donley Ranch for a while to settle things, he would. He'd never settled someone's estate, their final affairs, and had no idea where to begin, but considering this was the only thing he could do for his brother, he'd figure things out. Maybe that preacher could be helpful after all.

Later. After he'd slept and looked around. After he had his legs under him again and his breath back in his lungs.

"Come on, pal." He patted his best friend and traveling companion. "Let's get you settled."

Hooking a finger beneath Freckles's halter, Levi led the appaloosa to a silver corral surrounding the old barn and turned him loose. The horse walked a few steps, head high and interested, and then broke into a celebratory run and buck. He'd spent most of three days in a trailer. He deserved to run free.

Levi didn't feel quite that joyful. A coat of paint

couldn't cover the barn's deep down ugliness. Maybe he'd burn the thing before the ranch sold.

After filling the water trough, Levi spun on his heel and headed to the house. His knees begged for rest. He had no idea what he would find inside his childhood home, but he was exhausted from the all-night drive and the emotion held tight in his chest. He couldn't wrap his head around the last three days. Scott. A wife. A baby. Emily.

Emily. What did she want? Why had she waited at his truck? Surely, not to rehash ancient history.

She was the last person in Calypso he wanted to see. Yet, she was the one he wanted to see the most.

"I'm losing it." He didn't even make sense to himself.

Emily was a long, long time and many miles ago.

Braced for what he would find inside the house, for a childhood that would slap him like the back of a hand, he pushed in the key and opened the door. A waft of scented air greeted him, something warm and homey like home-made cookies.

"Must be the wrong house." But he stepped inside anyway.

His knees wobbled. He blamed the old injuries, but memories poured in like a cloudburst, some good, too many bad.

The good ones were all of Scott, of a brother who somehow managed to find humor and mischief in otherwise long, endless days of farm labor.

Scott.

Levi grabbed for the wall to steady himself, eyes clenched tight as he took deep breaths. Slowly, he slid to the floor and sat for long moments, knees up, head down, listening for his brother's voice, his laugh, his whispered warnings that the old man was on a rampage, and Levi was in the crosshairs. Again.

He let the slide show of childhood flash through his head and wished for one more day, one more moment with his brother. In all their lives, no one in this house had ever said, "I love you." If he could do things over, he'd say the words to his brother... But he was too late. Scott was dead.

He couldn't grasp it. His brother, his only kin, *gone forever.*

Exhausted, he tilted his head back against the wall, where he must have dozed because when he opened his eyes, the room seemed dimmer. A familiar noise permeated the former quiet. Cows bawling. Probably hungry.

Who had been caring for them since...? Maybe no one.

Using a nearby sofa as support, he pushed to a stand, knees groaning. For Scott's sake, he'd take care of the responsibilities here. Cattle, horses, and maybe more. Pathetic that he didn't know.

As his mind cleared, he noticed the living room for the first time. Tidy, clean, and inviting, the once dark and cold space had been redecorated by someone. Certainly not his brother. A woman. Jessica, the sister-in-law he didn't know. Would never know.

A blue checkered throw was folded over the back of the off-white couch. Matching pillows made him want to stretch out and put his feet up. Homey. Warm.

Things had changed. But nothing could ever change enough to make him want to be here.

Levi moved around the room, noticing a cluster of photos on one wall where nothing had hung before. In one photo, Scott smiled so big he was all teeth next to a petite brunette with laughing eyes. Wedding photos. A picture of Scott working cows. Scott on horseback. The husband and wife in front of a Christmas tree.

Continuing through the lower rooms, he saw more changes, all of them adding a homey feel to the house that had never known one iota of warmth before. Light and sunshine. New drapes tucked open. Bright paintings. Religious wall plaques proclaiming Jesus as Lord.

Scott had married a woman of faith. Had she been the reason he'd joined a church? The knot in Levi's throat thickened. Had his brother found the good life at last?

He didn't know and probably never would, a fact that tormented him no end. He barely knew his own brother, the brother who had loved him and with whom he'd shared a bond of protection and brotherhood most siblings wouldn't understand.

Scott was gone, and Levi was alone. Not that he'd ever minded that before. Never minded leaving behind a job, a crew of cowboys, a woman now and then. But suddenly, here in this ranch house he'd hated for years, he was struck by how terribly empty his life had become.

"How's the baby?" Emily asked the moment she entered the sunroom of the Triple C Ranch.

Consuelo Galindo, chief cook and house boss of the

Triple C, and the only mother Emily had ever known, was watering her many plants. The small Mexican woman with the giant heart was Emily's go-to babysitter and resident grandma anytime Emily had a foster child in her care.

"He is sleeping now, but he fussed a long time. Poor little *bebe*." Dark face wreathed in sympathy, Connie set aside her watering can and glanced in the direction of the downstairs bedrooms. "Do you think he knows his *mama* and *papi* are gone?"

The question haunted Emily as it did with every infant who came into foster care. Did tiny Mason Donley yearn for the mother who would never return? Was that why he was fussy and restless? Was he missing the parents who loved him unreservedly?

Unanswerable questions and family tragedies made social work a sometimes grueling and heartrending line of work. But she was doing a good thing, helping children, and the pain was worth the gain. Kids needed advocates who really cared.

As the only social worker in Calypso, Emily was responsible for many displaced children, and tiny Mason was the latest. Given her friendship with Jessica, she'd loved this particular baby long before he'd come into care. He was special, and she'd be lying to say different.

"Thank you for watching him while I attended the funeral service."

Connie waved away the thanks. The Caldwell's surrogate mother adored kids and was frustrated that neither Emily nor her brothers had produced offspring for her to spoil. That Nate had recently married their neighbor,

Whitney Brookes, and was adopting her twin girls thrilled Connie no end. Emily was pleased about that herself.

"How was the service?" Connie asked as they started out of the sunroom and passed through the kitchen.

"Sad. Crowded. Half the town was there. I was glad Nate and Ace could make it. Whitney stayed home with the babies, but I understand that. She didn't know Jessica or Scott very well."

Emily stopped at the stainless-steel refrigerator for a water bottle. She offered one to Connie, who shook her head.

"Scott was a good neighbor and friend to us all. As Jessica was to you. Good people."

"The best." After a long swig of cooling water, Emily limped into the living room and plopped onto the leather sofa. "These heels are killing my feet."

She bit her lip and sniffled. Jessica Donley, her close friend and shopping pal, had given her the shoes when she'd been too pregnant to wear them. "I can't believe she's gone, Connie."

Connie sat next to her and offered a side hug. Emily rested her head on the slender shoulder she'd leaned on all her life.

"God's ways are hard to understand sometimes, *mija*. But we must not question. He is wise and good. His plan is perfect."

Emily wished she could agree. There didn't seem to be anything good or perfect about two young, healthy parents being killed in a freak flash flood. Nor about a tiny boy being orphaned.

She didn't argue, though. Like her three brothers, she loved and respected this wise little woman who'd come into their lives after their mother died. Emily had been a baby, the boys not much older when Dad had hired Connie. Now Dad was gone, too, but Connie remained, stalwart, steady, and loving, to take care of her *familia*, as she called the Caldwell siblings.

Connie's warm-hearted, giving example was why Emily had become a social worker and the reason she was involved in church and civic events. That and the fact that as a childless widow, Emily's home a short distance from the main house got very lonely.

"I tried to talk to Levi at the funeral."

Connie stiffened, her hand stilling on Emily's hair. "Oh, Emily. Is this a good idea?"

"I have to, Connie. Mason is an orphan, stuck in foster care until I find him the right home. Other than Levi, Ruby Peterson is the baby's only known relative."

"Ruby is a good Christian woman. But she is too old for a baby."

"And she lives in an assisted living center."

"*Si.* So sad for everyone. But Levi. I don't know about this. I do not trust that boy. He did wrong by you."

A heart scar Emily thought long faded began to throb.

"Levi had his reasons for leaving Calypso when he did." She and Levi were the only ones who really knew what had happened that long-ago day.

They were just kids, teenagers, but old enough to be madly in love. Or so she thought. Then she'd hurt him. He'd hurt her back. And he'd run away from her and

Calypso as fast as his battered old truck would take him.

"He broke your heart. You must be careful."

Emily managed a small laugh. "That was eons ago, Connie. A high school thing. Long forgotten."

"Maybe by you, but I do not forget the way he hurt you, my baby." She gave Emily's arm a squeeze. "Part of me is glad he left. Otherwise you would not have married Dennis. But, also, I remember you cried for days."

Months actually, but Emily kept that remark to herself. "I was seventeen, remember? I cried about everything."

Connie chuckled. "This is true. Remember how you cried until your *papi* let you spike your hair, and then you cried for a wig?" She shook her head in amusement. "Teenage hormones."

"Thank goodness I outgrew them." She hoped she'd also outgrown Levi Donley. "My only purpose in seeing Levi at all is for Mason's sake, certainly not because of some high school crush."

"I still do not trust him, but I will pray for him. Ruby says Levi travels too much. Like he is running away from something. He cannot settle down."

Maybe he was still running from the memories, from the father who'd made his boyhood a misery.

"Well, he has a place to settle now." The sore spot throbbed again. She hated that ranch. Had avoided it even after Jessica moved in. Now, the Donley Ranch belonged to the only other living person who'd been around that ugly day fourteen years ago.

"Do you think he will take over the ranch and stay in Calypso?"

Lord, she hoped not.

"No, I don't, and that brings us back to Mason. Levi is his closest blood kin. I have to talk to him about Mason's future."

"Can the county not send another social worker?"

"I won't ask for that! I don't want some stranger making decisions for Jessica's son. She was my friend. I *have* to make sure he's placed with exactly the right family. For Jessica's sake, as well as for Mason."

The chances of Levi accepting such an overwhelming, life-changing responsibility were slim. Very slim. He'd hated Calypso enough to leave and never look back, and according to Jessica, he and Scott rarely communicated. Which made the couple's request so much more bewildering.

"I'll lay out the options for him, but I'm confident he'll say no."

Which was exactly right in her book. A drifting cowboy who probably slept in his horse trailer had no business with a child.

Yet, Jessica and Scott had made their wishes clear on the day of Mason's birth, and the state also gave Levi preference. Even if the idea of seeing him bothered her more than it should have, and even if she completely disagreed with her friend's decision, she had a moral and professional obligation to see things through.

"When will you go?"

Emily straightened her shoulders. "As soon as Mason wakes up."

Connie was quiet for a minute. Emily recognized the silence. Connie would pray and consider before she offered an opinion. Finally, she nodded once. "*Si.* Levi must meet his nephew. It is right."

"Yes, he must. The law favors kinship. Plus, *I* know what Jessica and Scott wanted. It would be ethically dishonest of me not to share that information with Levi. Not to mention un-Christian."

"*Si. Si.*" Connie sighed. "I cannot understand why they chose him. He has been gone so long. He moves from one place to another. Ruby tries to keep up with his rambles, but he never calls or writes. That is not a good life for a baby."

"No argument from me."

"You would have been a better choice, *mija*, and I could be his *abuela*. I would like that very much."

As a child welfare worker, Emily never let her thoughts go there. She might want to, but she didn't. Conflicts of interest were frowned upon.

"Blood is thicker, as they say. Levi is kin. The law is clear, and he's the person Jessica wanted. But as Mason's social worker, I'm also obligated to tell him what I think is best for his nephew's future. I have a stack of excellent paper-ready families yearning for a baby."

Emily's palms had begun to sweat. She rubbed them up and down the sides of the condensing water bottle. She hadn't been to the Donley Ranch since the day Levi left town. Not even to visit Jessica, and her friend, bless her, had never questioned Emily's aversion to the place. Jessica probably thought she still carried a torch for Levi and couldn't bear the reminders.

Connie smiled and patted her arm. "He will agree. You will convince him. Babies are *muy* hard work."

"Exactly the reason I'm taking Mason with me. I want Levi to understand the enormity of parenting a child and to realize that he has other, better options."

Levi had a child's future in his hands. So did she. And she was determined to do the best thing for Jessica's baby.

3

L evi stomped his boots at the back door and entered the quiet, empty house, so weary he could drop in his tracks and sleep on the cool mudroom tile. The livestock, however, came first, a rule that had been drilled into him as a boy. No matter how tired, hungry, sick or cold he was, Dad had pushed him out the door to care for the animals day and night from the time he was four years old.

Truth was, his stomach hurt too much to eat, and he wasn't confident he could actually sleep if he tromped up the stairs to his old room. He hadn't been up there yet. Maybe he'd sleep on the couch in the pleasant room created by his brother's wife. Or maybe he'd bunk in his trailer.

In the kitchen, he drew a tall glass of water and washed down dust mingled with sorrow. From the corner of his eye, a flash of shiny bronze snagged his attention. He turned toward the window next to the round table for four. Same table from his childhood except someone had refinished the chairs and added a bright blue tablecloth and yellow flowered placemats. Smack in the middle, a fake sunflower poked up from a small vase. Put there by a woman who would never see them again.

He stroked his fingers over the back of one chair and tugged the ruffled window curtain to one side. The front yard needed mowing. Another item for a chore list he had yet to make.

A car turned down the driveway and slowly approached the house. The heart he'd thought had stopped at the cemetery thudded painfully to life.

Emily. Again. What did she want? Didn't he have enough guilt and shame to deal with? Why couldn't she leave him to grieve in peace?

He watched her exit the shiny late-model SUV. She straightened her dark skirt, the same one she'd worn at the cemetery. As if she had to muster courage, she stood perfectly still, some kind of manila folder under her arm, and gazed at the house. He got that. This place held a nightmare for her too. He didn't blame her for any of it. The fault was his.

Over and done, cowboy. Move on.

But seeing her again brought the shame back as fresh as this morning's funeral. Even with shorter hair and with fourteen years added to her age, Emily looked as beautiful as ever standing there in the faded evening. A man didn't forget some things, no matter how far he ran.

He dropped the curtain and went to the front door. Outside he heard a car door slam. Then another. Curious, he stepped out onto the porch. She toted a baby carrier in her left hand.

So, she'd had a baby. What did he expect? By now, she and her husband probably had several kids.

Why was she here? Certainly not for a friendly reunion of high school sweethearts. Certainly not to rehash their break-up.

He squinted, looking as unfriendly as he knew how, which wasn't too difficult given the situation. "What do you want?"

"We need to talk." She didn't seem intimidated by his bad mood. The teenage Emily would have gotten flustered. Not this Emily, though from her taut expression and shifting eyes, she didn't want to be here anymore than he wanted her to be.

Levi leaned a shoulder against the porch post and folded his arms. "So, talk."

She hitched her chin, drawing attention to a tiny white scar beneath, the one he'd loved to trace...and kiss. He'd been with her the day she fell, landed on a sharp rock, and needed four stitches. She'd wanted him to go to the emergency room with her. The old man wouldn't let him.

To shake the thought, he glanced aside, but the memory lingered.

"Inside, if you don't mind," she was saying. "Mason may only be three weeks old, but this car seat gets heavy."

His insides seized upward and obliterated all thought of Emily's soft, white skin. Mason? Scott's son was in that carrier? What was Emily doing with him?

He stepped to the side and pushed the door open

with one hand. Without a word, she sailed into the living room. A subtle scent like apple blossoms trailed behind, tickling his nose. In spite of his determination to steer clear of Emily Caldwell, he inhaled and held the fragrance next to his heart.

Less than five minutes in her company and she was messing with his head.

He wanted her gone. Gone, so he didn't have to think about what he'd done, who he was. Gone so he could hide from the humiliation. She was too much of a reminder of everything he'd spent fourteen years trying to forget.

She stopped in the middle of the living room and turned to face him, the baby carrier swinging from one hand. She looked nervous. Good. She'd leave faster that way. She glanced at him and then away, but in that nanosecond of eye meeting eye, he saw the past and pitied her. She'd loved him, and he'd failed her magnificently.

Hot regret burned his conscience. Maybe he should apologize, but he'd never learned how. And after all this time, surely she no longer thought about him or that awful day.

He thrust a hand toward the couch. "Might as well sit down."

She turned away slightly, but her gaze lingered on the wall photos of Mason's smiling parents before she lowered the carrier to the black-and-white rug and took a seat.

"He's asleep. Do you want to see him?"

Yes. No!

His pulse kicked in as if he'd stepped up on a wild mustang for the first time.

"Why do you have Scott's baby?" He folded his arms again and leaned against the wall, as far away from her and the child as possible.

"I'm a social worker for Calypso County family services. Mason is in my care until permanent arrangements are made."

Social worker. The career choice fit her. Even as a teenager, Emily fretted about the less fortunate and rallied friends to help with her latest volunteer project. Him included, though he'd had to sneak away from the ranch and give up sleep to do it. He hadn't wanted to let Emily down. Then he had.

But she wasn't here to revisit a teenage love affair. Neither was he.

"Permanent arrangements with who? Jessica's family?"

"Jessica had no family."

He titled his head, troubled by the revelation. Jessica had no one. Scott had no one. "What will happen to Mason?"

She looked at him for a second and then glanced away. "Ideally, he'll be adopted by a loving couple. We have several excellent applicants who would love to be his parents."

Good people who couldn't have kids. Who wanted kids. Sensible, even if the idea settled in his belly like curdled milk. "Who decides things like that?"

Stunning cat-green eyes locked on to his. He got a

creepy feeling, the kind that said he wouldn't like what she had to say. And that maybe she didn't like it either.

"You do."

The quietly spoken words blasted around the walls of his skull. Him? He would decide the future of a little baby he hadn't even known existed until this morning? "I don't understand."

"To be completely honest, neither do I, but that was their wish. Scott and Jessica named you Mason's guardian on the day he was born."

A bolt of electricity shot through him. A baby's guardian? Him? "Why didn't I know this?"

"There wasn't...time." She pressed her lips together.

Sorrow pierced him like an arrow. Scott had run out of time. The best man Levi had ever known wouldn't be here to raise his boy.

His glance slid toward the mysterious, canopy-covered baby seat. "Then, I guess I'm not his *legal* guardian?"

"No."

Was that relief or disappointment he felt? He wasn't sure. What he did know was that his whole world had turned upside down, and Mason was part of the tumult. "So, why are you here?"

"Jessica was a close friend. I was there the day Mason was born, and they told me their wishes. I'd be dishonest not to share them with you."

"Your strong moral compass is still intact, I see."

Her slim shoulders stiffened. "Some people have ethics, Levi."

Ouch. Sweet and gentle Emily had grown claws.

She held up her left hand like a stop sign, and Levi did his best not to notice that she wore no wedding band. But the thought was there in the back of his brain and made him wonder. No woman as incredible as Emily could have remained unattached.

"That was uncalled for," she said. "Forgive me. This is a horrible day for you, and I am so very sorry for your loss."

Levi cleared his throat but had no words. *Don't talk about Scott. Don't talk about the funeral. Just don't.*

To his relief, she didn't.

"The point that you and I must address right away is Mason's future."

Like he knew anything at all about babies. "Okay. How does this work?"

"Even if they didn't have time to complete the necessary paperwork, Jessica and Scott chose you as guardian. We're still searching for others, but as near as I can ascertain, you are his closest relative. This means you have first option of rights anyway. That's the law. Then, if you opt out, you can either let the county decide his future or you can look through the adoption applications and help me choose a family for him."

If you opt out. As if a child were a box to check or an app he didn't want to download.

"Scott wanted me to raise his son?" He couldn't seem to get past that truth.

"I'm sure you'll want to do what's best for Mason and allow him to be adopted by a loving couple." She fiddled with the lapel of her jacket and avoided looking at him. He understood. He was a bad memory. So was she. But she was a good one too. Lots of good ones. "Children need stable, healthy families, Levi. I brought the papers for your signature."

He heard what she wasn't saying. What her social worker ethics and innate courtesy kept her from saying. But her feelings came through loud and clear. Levi Donley, the spawn of a despicable man, was too irresponsible, too worthless, to be anybody's parent, and if he cared for Scott at all, he'd let her and the county choose a real home, a real family, for baby Mason.

The fact that she was probably right wasn't lost on him.

But Scott hadn't agreed. He'd wanted his son with family. He'd wanted Levi.

Like a sleepwalker, Levi moved toward the brown-and-blue carrier and crouched beside it. His worse knee screamed. He ignored it.

Hand trembling, he gently pushed back the canopy and gazed down into the sleeping face of his brother's baby boy.

Scott's son.

An overwhelming sense of awe struck him like a blow. This tiny human was Donley blood. *Levi's* blood. A genetic link to everything he was, everything he could be, everything he had been. His and Scott's past, and all Scott had left of the future, lay sleeping beneath a blue baby blanket.

Levi cleared his throat, shaken.

A sense of connection such as he'd never experienced drew him to the infant. Like a train vibrating the earth from far away, a deep internal rumble shook him hard. To cover the emotion and ease his knee pain, he sat on the floor next to the baby carrier and gazed in wonder at his sleeping nephew.

Earlier today, the baby had been little more than an abstract thought. Now he was real. A tiny person. Kin.

Suddenly, the decision went from simple and sensible to enormously complex. Whatever Levi decided would affect this child forever.

Stretching out an unsteady finger, Levi stroked a cheek as velvety soft and as warm as a horse muzzle. Had he ever touched a baby before? If he had, he didn't remember. But he would remember this.

Mason squirmed, his little mouth puckering though he never opened his eyes. Emboldened, Levi smoothed the barely-there cap of brown hair with his fingertips, studied the tiny button nose, the slash of brown eyebrows, the heart-shaped chin with a dimple like his own. Scott's boy. He must have been so proud of this handsome little critter.

A million thoughts raced through Levi's head as he grappled with the enormity of this meeting.

Scott had made him responsible for his son. Stupid idea. Levi knew nothing about kids. He'd barely been one himself. He sure didn't know how to be a father. He was a footloose loner who couldn't lay claim to a thing but his truck, trailer, and horse.

And Scott's baby.

A little boy who would never know his daddy.

Levi's throat thickened. He passed a hand over his eyes as he stared down at the helpless infant. His only kin. His last living connection to his brother.

But he hated this ranch, this town. He couldn't stay.

The baby's eyelids quivered and lifted. Two navy blue eyes focused on Levi. The smallest fist he'd ever seen wobbled toward him. The fingers opened, stretched wide as if reaching. Levi placed his index finger against the little palm. Mason's fingers flexed tight around him, clinging.

The most amazing pleasure lifted inside Levi, swelling his chest. The tiny fist around his finger wrapped around his heart as well.

It struck him then. No one in the world cared where Levi Donley was. No one was waiting for him. No one but Mason. Scott had trusted his only brother with his greatest treasure.

Scott had believed in him.

"Do you want to hold him?"

Emily's voice jerked his head around. He'd almost forgotten her presence.

"I don't know how. I've never..." He lifted one shoulder in helpless entreaty. "Will you show me?"

She didn't look too happy about it, but Emily moved to the opposite side of the carrier and slid both hands behind the baby's back.

She looked at Levi above the canopy. "Support his back and head like this. He's getting some control, but his neck muscles aren't completely developed yet."

Levi followed her instructions from the opposite side, his hands feeling big and awkward against the small baby. His fingers bumped with Emily's. Her gaze flew up to his, and for a moment, they both froze. Fourteen years disappeared in a slideshow of memory. Emily laughing in the sunshine as she ran away with his hat, black hair flowing in the wind. Emily holding his hand when he'd had a rough day with his old man. Emily feeding him French fries with her fingers and promising to love him forever.

Forever hadn't lasted long.

"Maybe later," he mumbled, and withdrew his hands from beneath the infant. "I'm not good at this sort of thing."

Emily sat back on her heels, professional, though her cheeks glowed pink. Had she been remembering too?

"That's what I'm trying to tell you, Levi. A child is a huge undertaking, and you have no experience with kids."

"None."

"Don't feel badly about that. Plenty of people aren't ready for parenthood, especially under such unexpected and tragic circumstances." Her tone was soft and persuasive. "All I need is your signature rejecting guardianship, and we'll choose a wonderful, loving family for Mason. If you're interested, I'll show you some applications, and you can help me decide."

She was giving him a way out. He could put the ranch up for sale, get in his truck, and head to anywhere he wanted to go. Like always.

"What about Aunt Ruby? She's related. Is she still—?" He couldn't talk about death on a day like this.

Emily smiled. "Your great aunt is very much alive and doing pretty well for someone in her late eighties. She moved into an assisted living facility in Calypso a few years ago after a fall and doesn't get around very well anymore, so I don't think she's the answer for Mason."

Of course. What was he thinking? Aunt Ruby had seemed old when he was a kid.

He flicked a glance at tiny, innocent, helpless Mason. His nephew. Scott's boy.

Blood roared in his head. His pulse sped up until he imagined a doctor slapping his chest with those paddle things.

Mason was waiting.

"No."

Emily's dark head tilted quizzically. A small gold earring glinted. "Excuse me?"

"No. I won't *opt out*." Was he losing what was left of his mind?

"But—"

"Scott wanted me to care for his boy, so"—Levi licked lips gone drier than the Mohave and swallowed back all the reasons he shouldn't do this—"I'm willing to give it a try."

EMILY BRISTLED, warm cheeks growing hotter by the minute, and not because touching Levi had stirred her emotions. Even if it had. Right now, she wanted to slug the man. Of all the idiotic, irresponsible comments she'd heard in her years as a social worker, this one took the grand prize.

"You'll *give it a try?*" Incensed, she leaped to her feet and took two paces away before she did something violent. And she had never done one violent thing her life.

"This is a baby we're discussing, Levi, not a roping horse you can try out for a few weeks, and if he doesn't work out, sell him to some other cowboy. A child needs a permanent, stable family, not a rambling cowboy who didn't even care enough to remain in communication with his only sibling."

Emily put a hand over her mouth and froze, aghast. What was wrong with her today? Why had she allowed Levi to push her usual kindness and professional control off the cliff? The man had lost his brother, for goodness sake!

She took a deep breath, modulated her tone and tried again. More gently, she asked, "Did you even know Mason existed until now?"

"No." His voice was quiet, wounded. He kept his attention on the infant, though his shoulders stooped like an old man. "I should have."

Emily's conscience pinged. She was going about this all wrong. He was hurting. She was hurting. They'd hurt each other. Nothing about this day or this meeting was even remotely good.

"I'm sorry for all of this, Levi. Sorry to spring this on you today of all days, but you have to realize that expedience is important." She lifted her palms imploringly. "Mason is a three-week-old baby. Are you ready to deal with that?"

Levi stroked his index finger over Mason's hair and didn't reply. She could practically see the wheels turning inside his head. He had no answers.

Emily spoke softly, entreating him to see things her way. The right way. "Don't you think Mason deserves a mother and a dad who are already prepared? A committed couple eager to take on the responsibility? Jessica was my closest friend. I want the best for her son."

She didn't say the rest. Levi wasn't the best choice, no matter what his brother and sister-in-law had said during a misguided fit of emotion after Mason's birth.

Levi looked up at her, his chin cleft a reminder of the times she'd put her finger there. He would grin and say, "A perfect fit."

But they hadn't been, just as he was not the best fit to raise Jessica's baby.

He nodded, looking so sad and tired, she wanted to comfort him. "Let me think about this, okay? I'm a little overwhelmed right now, and my brain is fuzzy. I haven't slept much. Tucson's a long drive."

Her conscience pinched harder. How long since he'd slept? Ate? He'd buried a brother today. The Levi she remembered couldn't express his feelings very well, but he had to be devastated. "Of course."

Her timing was terrible. She should have waited a few days and given Levi more time to grieve and to settle in before confronting him with an orphaned nephew and a handful of papers to sign.

But she'd been afraid he'd disappear.

"I'll leave the paperwork on the coffee table. Look at it later. Whenever you feel up to it."

"Okay."

She hooked an imaginary stray hair behind one ear. "My contact information is on my business card. I'll leave that too."

Levi stroked the top of Mason's head over and over, touch light and gentle, tender even. His expression was unreadable. "What about him? Who'll look after him while we figure this out?"

"I will. Connie helps when I'm working."

He almost smiled. "Connie's a good woman."

The Donley boys had never known a mother's love. All they'd had was Slim Donley, a slave-driving, cold, hard-hearted excuse for a father. A certifiable ogre.

Again, she yearned to reach out to Levi. She was a sucker for the hurting.

"I should go."

He needed rest. And she needed to put some distance between them and get her head together. He'd rattled her and caused her to react in a completely inappropriate manner, though she couldn't understand why. Fourteen years was a lifetime. They were different people now.

Resuming her professional role, she reached down for the baby. Levi rose and brought the carrier up with him. "I'll carry him out for you."

"No need."

She might as well have saved her breath. He led the way to the orange Rogue.

"Put him in the backseat. State law."

He set the carrier inside, facing forward. She leaned around him to turn it around. He smelled like hay and fresh air.

"Another state law. Infants face the back for safety."

Even as she spoke, she realized she was reminding him that he knew nothing of caring for an infant. For his sake and Mason's, Levi must come to realize the job was too much for him. He was not daddy material.

She buckled the baby in and turned to find her door open and waiting. Nearly six feet of cowboy held it open the way he'd done hundreds of times. Quiet. Patient.

"Thank you." She tucked her skirt and slid onto the seat.

"Emily."

She started the car, aware of damp palms against the steering wheel. "Yes."

"I want to do right by him. I want to do right by my brother too. I owe him that."

Levi stepped back and closed the door with a soft snick.

As she drove away, she glanced in the rearview mirror. He remained where she'd left him, alone and hurting, with Mason's future in his hands.

4

After Emily left, Levi was too exhausted and heartsick to do anything else. The animals would be fine until tomorrow, and he couldn't have eaten if his life had depended on it.

Rubbing a rough, cowboy's hand over his face, he climbed the stairs to his old room. His and Scott's. The old man had slept like the dead across the hall with the door shut, making nights Levi's favorite time as a boy. He and Scott alone in the upstairs room where they could talk about everything.

Some nights, they invented methods to escape the incessant work load their father piled on them. Few of their ideas ever panned out, but they reveled in the planning.

Idle hands are the devil's workshop. How many times had he and his brother heard that phrase, especially after Slim Donley had refused to let them join the baseball team or attend a movie with friends because they had chores to do? There was always work on the Donley Ranch. Even fishing had to produce food for the table.

No one remained idle long around Slim, especially the Donley sons. Levi had been driving a tractor by himself at the age of six. Driving an old farm truck at eight.

He hadn't minded the chores. Not really. Hard work never killed anyone, and by the time he was a teenager, Slim was farming him out to other ranches to earn his own money. He had been thrilled to buy boots, clothes, and eventually a truck. Other ranchers, especially over at the Triple C, were a lot friendlier than the old man.

Levi loved ranching. It was the lack of free time, the lost childhood, the thankless, grueling expectations of a father who seemed to resent the food he ate, the air he breathed, his very existence.

At the top of the stairs, Levi paused to rub his knee and noticed more changes. Walls once dull and lifeless were painted a creamy color and brightened with a collection of framed sunrise-sunset photos. Had Jessica taken the pictures?

When he reached the bedrooms, one on each side, he stared at the old man's door and decided not to open it. Not tonight, though his mysterious sister-in-law had probably done a work in there, as well.

He pushed into the room that had been his and Scott's, finding more changes. Gone were the bunk beds and the tall dresser, along with the odds and ends of teenage boys. But what had he expected after fourteen years?

Apparently, Scott and his bride had made this room

their own. A queen bed atop a shaggy white area rug. Mirrored dresser. A single nightstand where a book lay open as if someone had put it down for only a moment, intending to return.

The sight tugged low in his belly, an ache that moved up into his chest and burned behind his eyelids.

Weary, heart-sore, he regarded the bed, and the tug grew stronger. The turquoise comforter was rumpled, an indention in the pillow. Had the new mother rested there with her baby and a book? Or had Scott napped in this spot that last fateful day?

He blinked away the images and went to the double windows, where dust had settled on the glossy white sills. Staring out at the night, he smiled a little to see the old window screen still intact, the aluminum bent at the corners. He and Scott would push out the screen and shimmy down onto the garage roof below, then make their escape under cover of darkness.

Though he could barely make out the silhouettes in the moonlight, below lay everything Scott had worked for. A new hay barn to the left of the old one. Corrals, catch pens, working chutes, and a fine herd of black baldies, a handful of horses and much more.

Now, it was up to Levi to figure out what to do with everything, including a living, breathing child.

He sighed, his breath fogging a spot on the window.

What *was* he going to do about Scott's baby? He was a cowboy, not a dad. His lifestyle was in the back of a trailer and on a horse's back. That was no life for a child.

But Scott had picked him.

He turned away from the starlit night and sat on the edge of the bed.

For now, he needed to sleep. If he could.

He bent forward and grasped the heel of his boot. From beneath the bed protruded a pair of brown, worn work boots, laces trailing. Scott's boots.

Scott had been the one to lie down on the pillow, to read the book on parenting, to leave one final indention to prove that he had existed.

Levi's chest squeezed so hard he grew breathless for a second. Was this the way a panic attack started? Chest tight, pulse pounding, stomach heavier than a load of bricks?

He'd expected his brother to always be here when and if he decided to return.

Life didn't simply end. It left behind the messy details.

With a soft thud, his boots dropped to the shaggy white rug. One boot tipped over against Scott's. He left it, along with his clothes, in a pile on the floor. Too tired to do anything more, he snuffed the light, tugged the soft comforter aside and settled in on Scott's pillow.

As he stacked his hands behind his head, a hundred thoughts darted through his mind. He imagined he could hear Scott's whisper from the top bunk that was no longer there, the smile in his voice, the soft laugh that said he was up to some mischief. Somehow Scott had never lost his sense of humor.

Emily either. Emily had cheered him, made him laugh, made him feel like a normal boy instead of his old man's workhorse.

She hadn't been laughing today.

He tossed to one side, aching in the darkness, the quiet around him so profound he could hear the buzz of silence.

He tried to think about his last job in Tucson and the red-haired boss's niece who'd favored his company. He'd liked her, but he hadn't loved her.

Not the way he'd loved Emily.

Though he'd long ago put her in a mental lock box, tonight Emily wouldn't stay out of his head. Emily and Scott and a tiny boy with a dent in his chin.

She was a social worker, a champion for kids. He was proud of her.

Was there a man in her life? A husband? A woman like Emily deserved a good, steady man who could make her as proud as she made him. Someone who wouldn't let her down and run away when bad things happened.

He should have looked at her business card to learn her last name. Couldn't still be Caldwell. But he hadn't wanted to think about the papers she had asked him to sign. His head was too fuzzy, too out of focus.

Duty had forced her to come to this ranch and talk to him. How she must have resented coming here. Resented him.

But she cared about baby Mason.

So did he.

He heaved a noisy, frustrated sigh and shifted positions one more time.

Sleep, Donley. Sleep.

Tomorrow would be soon enough to figure out the rest of his life. The rest of Mason's.

Levi! Get your lazy carcass out of bed before I climb these stairs and drag you out.

Levi's eyelids shot open. He leaped up from the cushy bed, grappling at the side for his jeans. "Coming, Dad. I'm coming."

Heart bounding, he jammed his arms into the rumpled shirt and grabbed his boots, hopping on one foot as he started down the stairs.

The last thing he wanted was to start the day off with the old man in a bad mood. Bad mornings meant back-breaking days and more verbal abuse than any kid should have to hear.

He was halfway down the stairs when full conscious-ness cleared the cobwebs. Dad wasn't waiting below. Dad was dead.

He must have been dreaming.

Slowly, Levi slithered down onto a stair step and sat there with a boot dangling from one hand. Scott was dead, too.

He was here on Scott's ranch, but his brother was gone forever.

Unexpected anger welled up like a geyser. Raring back like the baseball pitcher he'd never gotten to be, Levi threw the boot with every bit of strength he could muster. The brown Justin Roper thudded down the stairs, raising a racket in the silent house, and came to a rest at the bottom.

Levi dropped his head into his hands. He couldn't do this. He didn't belong here. He needed to get in his truck and escape. Now. As fast as he could. Put the ranch up for sale and hit the road.

Leaving was what he did best.

But how did a man escape his brother's memory? His death? And the fact that he'd left behind, not only a ranch, but a son?

As anger seeped out like air from a punctured tire, despair moved in to ride his shoulders. He pushed off the stairs and hit the showers. Get dressed. Do the work. Work numbed the mind and took the edge off. He hoped.

By the time he stumbled downstairs to the kitchen, he'd grown an appetite. The clock on the back of the stove announced nine o'clock, a shock since he hadn't slept that late in years. No wonder he was finally hungry.

He opened the refrigerator, one of the nice ones with filtered water and ice in the door. Slim Donley would have called it a lazy man's appliance. He could practically hear the old man now. "Anyone too lazy to open a door and get their own ice doesn't deserve to drink."

Not that they couldn't afford the upgrades, but Slim thought everything had to be done the hard way. Especially if the hard way taught his sons the meaning of real work and where a dollar came from.

"Score another for Scott." Levi smiled a little as he removed a carton of milk and sniffed. He winced and turned his head aside. Spoiled. Sour.

What else had gone bad in the days since...?

He swallowed the uncomfortable knot and pulled out three small containers. Opening the lids, he found meatloaf, some sort of casserole, a bowl of potatoes.

Leftovers Scott would never finish. Leftovers his wife

had lovingly placed in pretty lavender bowls fully expecting to come back to them.

As Levi set the bowls and milk aside to discard, his appetite slowly retreated.

He found the coffee pot and brewed a pot full. While he waited for the drips and gurgles to end and the scent to wake him up, he opened cabinets and acclimated himself to the kitchen.

One entire cabinet was dedicated to baby bottles and other baby items he didn't recognize. He closed it, found a mug for his coffee, and stood with his back against the sink, sipping, thinking. Wishing he didn't have to think at all.

As a boy, he'd stood in this room and sat at that table hundreds of times. Today it looked inviting, not like before.

His gaze strayed to the bright place settings. Had the three Donley males ever had a happy family conversation over breakfast or supper? Had his father ever dispensed manly advice or talked to them like a father?

Not that he remembered. All he recalled was a glowering man bowed over his plate in cold, awkward silence. Sometimes, he growled orders for chores to be done or berated Levi for some foul up.

Had Scott changed all that? Had he built a good life here with his color-loving bride and their new son?

Oh, how he hoped so. One thing for sure, the sooner he was away from Calypso and these haunting memories the better.

Setting the cup in the sink, Levi extracted his cell phone and punched in a number. Jack Parnell, owner of the Long Spur Ranch outside Amarillo was waiting to hear his decision. Now, seemed the perfect time, and The Long Spur seemed the perfect reason to finish his business and get away from here.

After three buzzes, a booming voice answered. "Parnell here."

Levi dispensed with the niceties. "Jack. Levi Donley."

"Been waiting to hear from you," Jack said in his straight-shooting style. "What's the verdict? You coming to work for me and The Long Spur?"

"Yes, sir, if the job's still open."

"Best news I've had today." Parnell laughed, a rusty sound. "When can you get here?"

Levi raked his fingers through the top of his hair. "I need a few days, maybe a week. Something's come up."

"Oh? Trouble?"

"I'm in Oklahoma. The family ranch. My brother..." He paused, drew in a breath, stumbled over the hardest words he'd ever say. "My brother passed away. Flash flood."

Silence on the other end told of the other man's shock.

"His wife too. They left behind a new baby."

"Mighty sorry to hear that, Levi. What a tragedy! Anything I can do?"

"I need some time to get things settled. Put the ranch up for sale. Make some decisions for my nephew."

He gnawed his lip, fretting. Fretting about the job and the risk of delay, about selling the ranch, but mostly about his nephew.

Did he have any business taking on the responsibility

of an infant while he learned a new job that would require his attention day and night for weeks? Or was Emily right? Was adoption the best answer for Mason?

"Absolutely," Parnell was saying. "Take some time. A couple of weeks or so. My current manager doesn't leave until the end of the month. Will that work?"

"Yes, sir. Thank you. I appreciate the understanding."

"Do what you need to, son. A loss like that. I can't imagine." Parnell blew out a breath. "Keep in mind, though, it's spring, and you know what that means on a ranch."

"I do. I'll wrap things up here as fast as I can."

A couple of weeks should be more than enough. Levi doubted he could bear to stick around *that* long.

After another minute, they rang off, and Levi started out through the mudroom but stopped, frozen by the brown canvas jacket hanging on the far wall next to the washer. A Carhartt. The kind that shed rain and blocked wind. A rancher's friend against the elements. His chest squeezed. Scott's.

Levi went to the jacket, and though the weather was fine this morning, he slipped it on, wrapping himself momentarily in his brother.

He slid his hands in the pockets and found a paper in the right one. It was a note of some kind, folded and wrinkled if as someone had read and reread the message. Curious, he unfolded it. His pulse skittered to see a woman's handwriting. Jessica?

As he read the sweet words, his eyes burned. With loops and curls and a heart at the end, Jessica expressed her love for Scott and how eager she was to hold their baby in her arms. How thankful to God she was that He'd brought Scott into her life and how excited she was for their future together. Love oozed from the single, much folded paper.

A note written months ago, before Mason's birth. A note Scott had kept and read over and over again.

Carefully, Levi refolded the paper and slid it back into the pocket.

His brother *had* been happy. He'd been loved by the sweet woman who'd put her whole heart into a note Scott had clearly treasured.

Levi was comforted by the revelation, but tormented too. What good was all the love in this house when both people had been snuffed out before their time? When their son would never know them? Mason would never bask in the security of his parent's love for each other and him. He would never again be held in his mother's loving arms. He would never know his daddy's voice or be guided by his strong, competent hands.

Levi banged one tight fist against the washer. The metallic sound echoed as grief pushed down on him, too hard to bear. He banged again, teeth as tight as his fist.

"How could you let this happen, God?"

Scott and Jessica were Christians, weren't they? Shouldn't God love them best? Yet, they'd been denied the years to raise a baby they had clearly wanted. Little Mason was alone, left at the mercy of strangers.

Even *Levi* was a stranger, and Emily had made her opinion clear on that topic. He was the worst possible person to parent Mason. Though her rejection stung, Levi agreed with her.

But his brother hadn't thought so. Shouldn't Levi become Mason's guardian for that reason alone? Scott had never before asked anything from him, and he never would again. But he'd asked for this. He'd asked Levi to raise his son.

He crushed a fist against his chest.

Could he learn to be a dad when he'd never had a decent one? Could he juggle a new, demanding job and a baby?

If he accepted the responsibility, would he stop feeling like the worst excuse for a brother who had ever breathed?

He didn't know. All he knew was his brother had trusted him to be here when it mattered most.

After removing the coat, Levi hung it back on the peg and let his hand slide down over the rough duck material.

A good night's sleep had done little to clear his thoughts. If anything, he was more confused than ever.

5

I nside the modern, low-slung brick building of the Calypso County Department of Child and Family Services, Emily stacked four folders on her desk. These were portfolios of paper-ready couples eager to adopt a child, portfolios she'd had in her desk for months. Young couples who had waited and waited for a baby.

She'd personally met and vetted every couple during the application and home study process.

She flipped open the first folder and gazed at the Sinclairs' smiling photo before rereading their information. A fire fighter and a medical technologist who owned their own home and had a stable income, their references glowed. In seven years of marriage, they had suffered five miscarriages. *Five lost babies.* Her sympathy went out to this nice couple who longed for kids.

Satisfied that they were still as wonderful as she'd first thought, she put the folder to one side and perused the other three. All were good candidates. The issue was getting Levi to realize that *he* was not the right parent for Mason.

Emily propped an elbow on her desk and glanced out at the street, where traffic moved at a snail's pace through the town of Clay City, Calypso's county seat. A late model silver pickup truck rumbled past, reminding her of the handsome cowboy.

Levi had looked haggard yesterday, a pallor beneath his naturally dark skin. She still felt guilty about dumping so much on him on the day of his brother's funeral. She was rarely so insensitive and had never behaved in such an unprofessional manner.

Was her friendship with Jessica clouding her objectivity? Or was her problem the good-looking cowboy himself?

She sighed and pulled a granola bar from her desk.

Simply hearing his voice had brought back memories of their youthful love and that painful time when everything went south. He'd been her first love, her first kiss, and they'd had such romantic plans for the future. Marriage, kids, a ranch of their own. A future, of course, that never happened.

Now she didn't even know the man. She knew his face and his voice, the cleft in his chin and so much of his past, but she didn't know *him*.

She did, however, understand grief and loss, and Levi had a boat-load right now. When Dennis had been killed, she'd thought her world had come to an end. Somehow, God had carried her along until she was able to breathe again and find beauty and meaning in life once more.

As she chewed the granola bar, she wondered about Levi. Did he know the Lord? He hadn't in high school, though he'd been tolerant of her strong religious views.

Sometimes he'd teased her, called her his Saint Emily, but he'd never gone to church with her. She blamed Slim Donley for that. Weekends rarely offered time off for the overworked Donley boys.

Where had Levi been for fourteen years? Word drifted back through the rumor mill that he rambled from ranch to ranch and town to town, never settling anywhere. Why was that, she wondered. Had he missed Calypso and his brother? Had he missed her?

She caught the thought and examined it. *Missed her?* What in the world was going on her in head today?

As she tossed the bar wrapper into the trash, she also tossed away the silly idea. She knew better to revisit her history with Levi. Hadn't done it in years. Not since she'd met Dennis.

She'd loved her late husband, and when he'd died, love had died with him. She didn't trust love anymore. Not the romantic kind. Love always seemed to leave her, whether by truck or by death, and the hurt was too deep to take another chance.

Levi had looked so broken, and she was a natural born rescuer.

After a swig from her ever-present water bottle, Emily gathered the four file folders and started out of her cubicle. Levi Donley was only in her life again because of her job and her dedication to Mason. End of subject.

As she turned to leave, her county supervisor came into view. In immaculate suit and tie, Tim Myers looked like a tough boss, which he was, but he was as fair as he was professional.

"Where are you headed?"

She motioned to the folders. "I'm going over these adoptive applications for the Donley baby. I think it's important for bonding to place him as soon as possible."

"Couldn't agree more. No success in locating a relative?"

The question gave Emily pause. A relative wasn't the best thing for Mason. Not *that* relative. "Well...there are two so far, but one is elderly and in assisted living. I'm still searching."

"What about the other?"

"I don't think he'll work out. He's a cowboy accustomed to moving around a lot. I doubt he's suitable."

"Why not?"

She shifted, hedging. No way she'd dump her teenage heartbreak on Tim. He wouldn't understand, and she couldn't explain what any of that had to do with Levi's suitability as a parent.

"He's a drifter, from what I understand, with no real roots. I don't think Levi Donley is prepared to parent a child."

"Have you spoken with him? Met him?"

Oh yeah. Many, many times. "Yesterday."

"How did he react?"

"He seemed stunned, uncertain. My timing was off, certainly. He'd just buried his brother, but I'm convinced he doesn't want the responsibility."

"Did he say that exactly?"

"No." He'd said he'd *try*. Thank goodness, he'd

backed away and asked for more time to consider.

"As you said, bad timing, but sounds like we're talking about an uncle. That relationship is meaningful."

"Yes, but..."

Tim adjusted his tie, always a sign that he had something boss-like to say.

"Family bonds are important to keep intact." When she started to argue, Tim stopped her with a raised palm. "You're one of my best, and you know the protocol. The state encourages kinship adoption if at all possible to keep family bonds intact. Talk to the uncle again. Run the background checks. If his character pans out and he's agreeable, he's the baby's best option."

No, he wasn't! But Emily kept that thought to herself. She'd already raised flags with Tim, and it was imperative she be the social worker to decide Mason's future. She loved the tiny child. No other staff member could say that.

"I'll talk to the uncle again."

A few minutes later, she left the office, stewing as she drove the twenty miles back to Calypso. What kind of life could Levi give a child? Sleeping in the back of a trailer? Moving every few months? What if he grew tired of child-rearing and simply took off?

She wouldn't be much of a social worker if she let that happen.

Deciding the granola bar would do until dinner, Emily skipped a real lunch to stop at the post office and then the grocery store to pick up snacks for a women's meeting tonight at church.

While she drove the few blocks to the Evangel

Church, she spoke with Connie on Bluetooth. Juggling Mason's care and her heavy case load with community and church responsibilities kept her hopping, but Mason came first.

"Mason is on my lap right now," Connie said. "He's a hungry little hombre today but much happier."

The smile in Connie's voice heartened Emily. "My supervisor wants me to talk with Levi again, so as soon as I stop by the church and get things set up for tonight's meeting, I'll come get Mason. I think the more Levi sees him and realizes how a baby changes a person's whole life, the more likely he'll want no part of it."

"Is this comfortable for you? To see so much of Levi Donley?"

Comfortable? Not even close. "I'm a big girl, Connie. I deal with people every single day. I can take care of myself."

"So strong and independent." Connie laughed softly. "Exactly like your father. I'll have Mason ready when you arrive."

Emily rang off as she pulled through the circle drive and parked beneath the awning of Evangel Church. Though a modern metal building without much character, the interior of the church was warm and welcoming and provided plenty of room for meetings and future expansion.

The pastor's office was located right inside the front glass doors. He met her in the foyer and took the grocery sacks from her. "Saw you on the security camera."

Emily smiled and followed him down the hallway to the back of the building and the fellowship hall. Pastor

Marcus Snider was close to her age, but his time in seminary, coupled with a tour in the military, made him wise and thoughtful beyond his years.

He plunked the snack bags on one of the round folding tables. "Nate and Whitney were in earlier and set up the tables for tonight's meeting."

"Nice of them. Whitney does such a pretty job with the centerpieces." She trailed her fingers over the pots of bright spring flowers. They made her think of Jessica and her eye for beauty, the way she could snap a random picture with her phone and turn it into a piece of art.

The pastor tilted a hip against one of the tables and crossed his muscled arms.

"How you doing, Emily? Tough week."

The softly spoken question was full of concern. That was Marcus. Get to the heart of the matter with compassion and a genuine desire to help. He knew how close she and Jessica had been and how hard this accident had hit her.

"Most of the time, I'm fine. I'm not even sure the reality has fully sunk in." She rubbed the sore place above her heart. "It happened. She's gone. I can't change that. I wish I could, but questioning God's will is pointless."

"But you do?"

"Yes. I do." She studied the back of her ringless left hand, remembering the shock and grief of Dennis's accident. And now Jessica. "I shouldn't. I'm sorry."

"We all struggle with this kind of tragedy, Emily. God understands. He's not mad at you. Our Heavenly Father thinks in terms of timeless eternity, but we humans are stuck in this finite box called life. We're short term. He's forever. Our brains won't hold something that big." He shifted. "Just remember, God knows you're hurting, and He cares."

Emily raised watery eyes. "Thank you for not telling me how much better off they are in heaven. I know that, but losing them still hurts."

"Platitudes are pretty useless. Sometimes all we need is a listener, and I'm always up for that." He straightened and dropped his arms to the side. "Anything else I can do to help?"

"Pray."

"Got you covered there. I'm praying for Mason, too. The whole church is. It's hard to think his dedication was only two weeks ago."

Emily managed a smile. "Jessica and Scott were practically bursting with pride."

"Great day. Terrific after party. A good memory to hold on to." Marcus motioned toward the attached kitchen area. "Got time for coffee?"

She shook her head and started into the kitchen. "Maybe a water to go. I'm headed out to the Donley Ranch to talk to Scott's brother about Mason."

Marcus followed, stopping at the coffee pot that he kept full for counseling sessions, workers, and anyone who dropped by. Like her. "Levi?"

She opened the huge stainless steel fridge. "You met him?"

"At the funeral yesterday. Briefly. Seemed pretty wrecked but holding it all in."

"That's Levi."

"You know him?" He shook a disposable foam cup from a tall stack and poured the coffee. The scent floated through the kitchen.

"Not anymore. Not really, but I used to, back in high school. He's been gone for years and years, never settled anywhere. Never kept in touch with his brother or anyone in Calypso. I don't expect him to stick around now."

"What about the baby?"

"Levi is not the right person."

"Why not? He's an uncle. I'm a pretty good judge of character, and Levi seemed like a decent guy."

Frustrated, she took out a water bottle and twisted the cap. Pastor sounded like her boss. The reminder that Levi was a relative was starting to wear thin.

"Maybe, but he's a footloose cowboy who apparently lives in his horse trailer or whereever he lands. He knows nothing about babies. He didn't even know Mason existed!" She looped a lock of hair over one ear. "So I'm going out there today to get him to relinquish any claim and let Mason be adopted by one of our applicant couples."

"Is that what Levi wants?"

"That's what's best for Mason." No matter what her supervisor thought. Yes, she would do as Tim directed and offer to run the background check, though she considered it futile because Levi would bolt soon anyway. He probably wouldn't stick around long enough for the paperwork to clear.

Light blue eyes studied her over a white foam cup. Pastor had that kind of stare, the kind that pierced right to the core of the matter.

"Sounds like you may not be giving the man a chance."

He didn't deserve one. The thought pinched her conscious. When had she become so judgmental and angry?

"Is there some reason you don't like the guy? Did he do something wrong that you know about?"

Besides breaking my heart? "We dated in high school, but that's long forgotten."

Marcus continued his gaze as if he didn't quite believe her. "Forgotten maybe. What about forgiven?"

Something pinged inside. Had she forgiven Levi? She thought she had.

"The relationship wasn't that big a deal, Pastor. A teenage romance. It's Levi's lifestyle that concerns me."

"Has he said he's leaving? That he's selling the ranch and heading for parts unknown?" Pastor fidgeted with his coffee cup. "Even if he doesn't remain in Calypso, does that make him ineligible to parent a child?"

"Well...no."

Pastor set his coffee aside. "Emily, you are an exceptional, caring social worker, a strong Christian who puts your whole heart into everything you do, a woman I respect and admire."

She could hear the *but* in his voice and braced herself.

"Jessica was your friend. You're still in shock and grief, like Levi. Is there any chance that perhaps you aren't seeing the situation as clearly as you normally would?"

Emily opened her mouth to protest but shut it again, silent. Pastor, for all his youth, was a wise counselor who saw more than most.

She *was* grief stricken. She *was* in terrible, painful shock.

"First of all, have you prayed about the situation?"

"I've prayed," she said, and then admitted, "but not the way you're asking. I've prayed Levi would sign the papers. I've prayed for the very best couple to adopt the baby."

"Ah. Then perhaps you should check your motives and try again. Are you certain you aren't pushing Levi to relinquish his rights because of your own feelings?"

"All I want is the best for Mason." She fiddled with the water bottle but didn't sip. Her motives were pure. Weren't they?

"All right, then, let's approach this from another direction." Pastor pressed his hands together in a praying gesture and tapped them against his lips. "Consider this: Maybe God put Levi in your path again for a different reason."

"To try my patience? To make me pray more?"

Marcus laughed. "Maybe. But maybe His reason has more eternal implications. How is Levi's spiritual life?"

Eternal implications. Hadn't she wondered if Levi knew the Lord? "I don't know. He seems...sad and lost."

Wasn't that normal after a death?

The pastor pointed his folded fingertips at her with a satisfied smile. "God's plan is almost never the one we would choose—trust me, I know this from experience— but He always knows best. Maybe He chose you to help, not only Mason, but Levi Donley as well."

And that was the last thing Emily had wanted to hear.

6

Levi jammed his boot down on the shovel and pushed hard. The smell of old hay and dried manure rushed into his nostrils. Scott had run the ranch alone, and from what Levi's trip around the three hundred acres revealed, the place was thriving but needed some upkeep. Not a lot, but enough to make a difference in the sale price. Money mattered, and this place owed him. Scott, too. Maybe he'd leave the money in a trust for Mason. Scott would like that. But to get the best price, he'd have to stick around long enough to make repairs and updates.

He lifted the shovelful of manure and dumped the contents in the wheelbarrow. The big, metal container, red paint long faded to rusty brown, was the same one he'd used a boy.

Last night, he'd dreamed the idiotic dream again, only this time when his father bellowed up the stairs in his scary voice, a smaller version of Scott had scurried into his clothes, heart thundering. The boy had been Mason.

Levi had awakened with an ache beneath his ribcage and the worry that he'd do the wrong thing. He'd hated his father, still did if he was honest, and being here brought back the feelings of anxiety and dread. He didn't want that kind of childhood for Scott's boy.

People in Calypso had hated the old man too. Mason shouldn't have to grow up with that kind of legacy hanging over his head either.

But the preacher said Scott was well liked, well respected. Could he have somehow vanquished the curse of Slim Donley?

This morning, Levi had driven into town to visit Aunt Ruby. She'd cried. He'd wanted to. The once vibrant Ruby was a tiny, fragile old woman who required the assistance of a walker. Her mind, however, was still sharp, and she'd made her opinion about Scott's baby clear. Donleys take care of their own.

Levi had already failed at that. With Scott. With Ruby. Would he do the same with Mason?

He swiped a forearm across his brow and mulled. His life had gotten way too complicated.

Out in the barn lot, Freckles whinnied to a pair of pasture horses. He and his mount were used to long days in the saddle. Long days of work and cows and wide-open spaces. Making camp. Sleeping on the ground.

How could he manage a baby?

He jammed his boot against another shovelful. His bum knee whimpered. Sweat beaded on his neck and back.

As he dumped the load into the wheelbarrow, he heard a door squeak open.

"Levi? Are you out here?"

His pulse jumped. *Emily*. He'd know that voice anywhere.

"In the third stall." He propped the shovel in a corner and pushed out into the barn's open alleyway. Behind him, the wooden door bounced a couple of times.

Emily stood in the open doorway gilded by a beam of sunlight, dust motes dancing around her. For a second, he was transported back in time. They were seventeen again, and his whole being leaped in delight to see her here. No amount of time could erase that feeling.

Then he noticed the baby in her arms and something entirely different stirred beneath his rib cage. That connection thing again. To Mason. To her.

"I wasn't expecting you today."

"I called. You didn't answer your phone."

He slapped at his back pocket. "Must have left it in the house." Or maybe he'd dropped it in a pile of manure. Wouldn't be the first time.

She remained frozen in the doorway as if afraid to come any further. Levi closed the distance between them. Like a deer about to bolt over the nearest fence, Emily clutched the baby to her shoulder.

"Is he asleep?" He reached for his nephew.

She drew back, expression as harsh as her voice. "Don't touch him. You're dirty."

Chastised, Levi's hand dropped to his side. What did she expect when she came into a barn?

"I'll meet you at the house." She spun around and rushed out.

The woman must despise him. And here he stood like a dummy thinking how beautiful she was and how right a baby looked in her arms.

He was seriously messed up.

Stomping mud and muck from his boots, Levi followed her across the yard. Halfway, he stepped in a hole and twisted his already throbbing knee. With a groan, he limped on.

Some days were diamonds. The past few had been stones.

The only bright spot had been a conversation with Miranda Bernstein, a local realtor. She was coming by this week to give him an appraisal. With a few repairs, the ranch should bring a good sum.

Entering the house through the back way, he stopped in the mudroom to wash up and change into a clean shirt —one of Scott's. His brother's clothes remained as he'd found them, carefully folded atop the dryer as if he or Jessica would return soon to put them away. Levi hadn't had the emotional strength to do anything with them.

Truth was, he didn't know what to do with any of Scott's things, including his ranch and his son.

He smoothed a palm down his chest, over the blue cotton. Wearing Scott's T-shirt hurt even more than his knee. But it felt good too.

He stuck his head into the living room. "Want something to drink?"

She shook her head. "This isn't a social visit. I brought some portfolios for you to look at."

The reminder stung. It shouldn't have, but it did.

The years hadn't brought forgiveness.

She hates your guts, Donley. Deal with it.

With a sigh, he filled a glass from the fancy refrigerator door and chugged the water before joining her. Though he did his best to hide the pain, his knee screamed. Emily already thought he was worthless. No use confirming it.

"Are you always this friendly with clients?" He crossed the space, trying not to limp.

She bit down on her lip, eyes widening. "Coming here is...difficult. The barn. Jessica."

Mention of the barn made the hair on the back of his neck rise. He latched onto the topic of Jessica.

"You were close to Scott's wife."

"Yes. Very. I see her everywhere in this house." Emily's rosy lips quivered a teeny bit. "The colors, those throw pillows, the photos."

Despite himself, Levi moved closer, the temptation to touch her strong. Emily was hurting. He'd never been able to stand seeing her upset. Maybe that was why he'd run in the first place. He couldn't undo what had been done.

"Me, too. About Scott, I mean. It's hard, but good too, Em. They were happy in this house."

Green eyes lifted to his. He and Emily were close enough to touch, but neither moved. Levi wanted to reach out. He wanted to give and receive comfort. But he couldn't. He'd always been bad at that sort of thing. She wouldn't want it anyway. Not from him.

He looked down at the baby in her arms, the tiny

reminder of why she'd come. Certainly not for a beat up cowboy with aching knees and an empty soul. She'd dreaded the trip, dreaded the stupid barn. No wonder she'd bit his head off and stormed out.

"Yes," she said softly. "I realize this is harder for you than for me. It has to be. Scott was your only brother."

Here was the Emily he remembered. Empathetic. Kind. Beautiful.

He felt as soft inside as Mason's skin. Emily did that to him. She'd always made him feel things.

"Em—" The apology he'd owed her for fourteen years stuck in his throat.

She stepped back, her shoulders tight, chin rising. "The sooner we get Mason settled, the sooner you can put all this behind you and move on with your life."

He blanched, stung. *Move on.*

That's why she was here. To convince him to go away.

For a minute there, he'd almost forgotten himself.

"Right. Sure. I get it." He rubbed the spot over his heart, the spot that never stopped hurting. "I want to hold him."

He could manage. He wasn't *that* useless. This was Scott's baby, and Levi had an enormous decision to make. For once in fourteen years, someone else mattered more than him.

When Emily hesitated, Levi held up both hands. "Clean. Clean shirt. I'm going to hold him, Emily."

She nodded. "As his uncle, you have that right."

Didn't she understand? This wasn't about rights. It was about the DNA he shared with this little human being. It was about the brother he'd failed so miserably.

No matter her opinion of him, he had to be sure his decision was the right one.

Awkward and more than a little anxious, he reached for his nephew. As Emily transferred the baby, her fingers grazed Levi's shoulder. This time he was ready for the electric charge. If Emily felt the jolt, she didn't let on.

"Put your hand against his back." Her tone had softened again. But not for him.

Levi slid his hand into place and spread his fingers wide. His hand seemed huge against the small body. "Brace his neck. I remember."

As if she expected him to toss Mason into the air and let him hit the floor, Emily remained close, one hand bracing the child. Levi had no objections. Being near her was a flood of good and beautiful through his weary soul.

"He's real soft." Holding Mason was doing things to his insides that he didn't understand, but he liked the feelings.

Was there more daddy material inside him than he'd ever dreamed?

Emily's lips curved. "Squishy."

Levi smiled, too, mesmerized by the child...and the woman.

"Yeah. Like he's boneless." Levi rubbed his cheek against Mason's head. "He smells nice."

"Connie bathed him before I picked him up. Baby lotion."

"Beats the cow manure I've smelled all afternoon."

Her gorgeous grin widened. "Only a cowboy would make that kind of comparison."

For the first time in days, Levi's spirits lifted.

Had they actually experienced a friendly moment?

"Does he sleep all the time?"

"A lot. Babies this young do. Fifteen hours or more."

He knew less than nothing about babies. Give him a calf or a colt and he was good.

The baby squirmed, his too-big-for-his-body head wobbling like a bobble doll. Levi braced the ultra short neck and watched, fascinated, as the little guy searched for something.

"What does he want?"

Before she could answer, Mason found his tiny fist. Loud sucking noises commenced.

Levi chuckled, heartened when Emily smiled too.

His warm fuzzies were short lived when Emily got to the point. "Have you thought any more about Mason's future? About adoption?"

Apparently, her smile had shark's teeth.

"Constantly."

"I brought the files of several prospective families for you to consider." She motioned toward a stack of manila folders near Mason's car seat. "I think you'll agree any one of them would be perfect for Mason."

They were back to that. She was bulldog determined to scoot him right out of Mason's life and right out of town. He didn't mind the latter. He was going anyway. But Mason was a different matter.

The pleasure of the last few minutes faded. His heart thudded painfully against Scott's shirt. "I can choose?"

"The court will make the ultimate decision, but they rely heavily on family wishes."

"I haven't agreed with this idea yet, Emily. What if I decide to raise him?"

She picked up the folders and fiddled with the edges. "Do you think that would be the best thing for Mason?"

There was the kicker. It probably wasn't. He should let Emily decide and keep his opinion, his feelings, out of it. The only reason she let him have any say at all was because of her commitment to Jessica and Scott. What did he know about such things? Nothing. Less than nothing.

But he knew how he felt when he looked into Mason's face and saw his brother. Leaving this boy would poke a hole in his soul that might never heal. He had too many of those already.

Yet, this wasn't about him. Mason was the one who mattered.

Carefully, he placed the infant in the carrier and gazed down into the perfect sleeping face. His heart dipped lower than a snake's belly. Could he sign away any opportunity to ever see that face again? Should he?

He pulled a hand over his mouth.

"Let's see those files."

IN THE KITCHEN, Emily spread the four file folders out on Jessica's blue tablecloth and tried not to look at Levi. In the living room just now, she'd gotten mushy and tender inside. A cowboy holding a baby was a sight to soften anyone's heart, but who was she kidding? Being near Levi stirred emotions long buried. Anger, hurt, love. That's what had her so rattled.

Out in the barn, she'd overreacted terribly. The moment she'd opened that door and smelled hay and horses, the memory assaulted her. That single event had changed everything, destroyed their dreams and separated her from the boy she loved.

None of that was Levi's fault, but she'd been uncharacteristically rude. Now she was pushing him away all over again.

Lord, help me. I'm doing this all wrong. I only want what's best for Mason.

But Pastor's words kept returning. What about Levi? Didn't he matter, too? Had she really ever forgiven him?

Did he feel as uncertain and lost as he looked? Was God using this tragedy for deeper purposes? And if he was, what were those purposes? And what was her part?

Emily knew Levi's past, knew the smoldering anger and hatred he'd harbored toward his father. Had he ever come to grips with that childhood wound? Had she?

She'd thought so, but had she?

She had a lot of praying in front of her. But right now, she had a job to do.

Clearing her throat, Emily flipped open a file. Levi stood at her shoulder. The scent of cotton shirt and recent soap surrounded her as he leaned in to study the photos and read the information. He was sincere, earnest, trying to do the right thing. The boy she'd known had been that way too.

She didn't want to remember that.

Everything about this situation confused her.

In spite of herself, she breathed him in.

Except for one, her memories of Levi were lovely. As a

couple, they'd been perfect together, a match made in heaven. Two ranch kids from a small town who loved all the same things, especially each other.

Then, after that ugly day, he'd disappeared. He'd left and never looked back. He hadn't even called. She couldn't forget that.

Tapping her index finger on the file in front of him, she drew his attention to the application. "Debra and Steven Banowski are wonderful people, Levi. All these couples are. They can give Mason everything, but most importantly, they can give him two stable, loving parents."

He turned his head her way, shadows in his eyes. The rescuer in Emily wanted to rush in and make things better. Not that she would.

They were as close as lovers, and as far apart as Earth and Jupiter.

"You know them?"

"I vetted each one myself." She tilted away from his tempting presence and shoved a curl behind her ear. "Mason's placement is extremely important to me. I've spent one-on-one time with each of these couples. I've seen them interact. I've talked to people who know them, and I have a very good instinct in these cases."

"No failures?"

"Not one."

"Okay." He sighed, his shoulders lifting as if he carried a heavy weight.

Emily knew what she was asking of him. She also knew he'd abandoned her, his brother, his home, and she

was afraid he'd eventually do the same to Mason. When
the going got tough, Levi got going.

As badly as she felt for Levi, Mason's well-being took
center stage. Those were good motives, weren't they?

From the living room came a mewling cry. Both she
and Levi spun toward the sound.

Emily moved first. "I'll get him. You go ahead and
look through those files."

LEVI WATCHED the beautiful social worker exit the
kitchen, his head pounding with indecision. She was
right. Any of these families would make great parents for
Mason. But were they the *right* parents for him?

What if he chose wrong? What if Mason grew up
lonely or abused or was turned into a workhorse the way
he and Scott were?

But Emily said these were great people, warm and
loving. The same could never have been said about Slim
Donley by anyone.

Levi rubbed at his chest, fretting, unsure. He trusted
Emily's judgment. She'd never given him any reason not
to. He'd been the failure, not her. And yet...

He flipped a page to a smiling blond couple. The
Sinclairs liked to ski and spent vacations in the moun-
tains. His bum knees meant he'd never so much as visit a
ski resort. The Westins owned their own business and
had a large extended family to give Mason cousins and
grandparents. He and Scott hadn't had anyone but Dad
and Ruby.

Next, there was Abby and Matt Priestly. They lived on

a farm with cows and horses and chickens and dogs. Mason could have pets, something Levi and Scott had begged for and never gotten. With the Priestly couple, Mason could grow up a country boy like his daddy.

If Levi kept the ranch, Mason could be a country boy here. He could have pets, a horse, a dog. All the dogs he wanted.

Levi shook off the thought. Wasn't going to happen. He hated this place. The best job in Texas awaited him, and he wanted it. All the perks without the hassle.

Mason could go with you. He could be a country boy there, too.

The idea held appeal, but was that the best situation for Mason? Hiring into a new position required time and commitment and long hours. How was that good for a baby?

He returned his attention to the file.

Yeah. He liked the sunburned Matt and sweet-faced Abby. Matt looked like a teddy bear, and Abby looked like a cookie baker. He'd always wanted a mom who baked cookies and gave hugs. Maybe he'd pick them.

The awful knot in his gut tightened to the point of pain.

What did he know about any of this? A week ago, he hadn't even known he had a nephew.

Now that he did, the responsibility was overwhelming. Scott had wanted him to raise Mason, but Emily ruled him out. And why shouldn't she? Why should she trust him with something as precious and fragile as a baby?

Emily was right. He couldn't be a daddy. Even now,

with this monumental decision in front of him, his first inclination was to hit the road.

Except the little boy crying in the living room held him with the power of an industrial-sized magnet. With Levi out of the picture, who would tell Mason stories of his father's childhood? Who would talk about Scott and keep his memory alive? Who would be able to point out the traits Mason shared with his daddy? With him? And how would the little man ever know how much his daddy had loved and wanted him?

Mason needed kin. He needed Levi.

People had kids all the time and still held jobs. There were babysitters, housekeepers, day care. It wouldn't be easy, but a determined cowboy could figure a way to make things work in Texas.

Quietly, shaking inside, he closed the folders and went to the doorway between the kitchen and living room. Emily sat on the couch, her head bent over Mason as she changed him.

"I've decided."

Her head jerked up. "Which couple?"

"None of them."

Her expression grew wary. "I don't understand. We have others, but those are all terrific."

"Agreed." He swallowed the knot. "Good people. I hope they get a baby, but it won't be Mason."

Slowly, head turned toward Levi, her eyes locked on his, Emily tugged Mason's blue onesie into place. "What are you saying?"

"If I sign away Scott's son, I won't have anyone." *Sign*

away. The words burned a hole in him. Somehow, he had to make her understand.

"This isn't about you."

"Maybe not, but he's my blood. Without each other, neither of us has family."

"He'll have a fantastic family, Levi. Any one of those couples will be his family forever. He'll be connected to them and everyone who comes after."

Levi exhaled in a frustrated gust.

He wasn't saying this right. He tried again to make her understand what he couldn't fully understand himself.

"Scott wanted *me.*" He tapped his chest. "Not strangers. Even really great strangers like those in there." He gestured toward the kitchen. "No one can give him what I can."

Her look was skeptical. "You're planning to settle down on this ranch for the rest of your life?"

"No. I won't." The very thought of being stuck here forever sickened him. "But I'll do my best for Mason."

Emily slapped the wet diaper into a baggie and reached for hand sanitizer. Mason lay upside down on her lap, his cheek against her knee, eyes closed as if a dry diaper was the only requirement for a life of contentment.

Life was a lot more complicated than that, as Emily's flashing eyes could attest.

She was ticked. He seemed to have a unique ability to infuriate the social worker.

"So." She bit off the words. "What you're really saying is, you'll stick with Mason as long it's convenient and as long as everything goes well."

His confidence wavered. "That's not what I meant."

"Exactly what *did* you mean?" She rubbed the pungent-scented sanitizer on her hands with enough vigor to start a fire. Mason jiggled but didn't wake up.

"I don't know how to explain. Mason is a Donley. It seems wrong for me to give him to someone else."

"Wrong for who?"

"Me. Mason."

"Adoption is a beautiful, blessed option. Even God loves adoption. It was his idea. He adopts *us* into His family when we accept Jesus."

She clapped her lips together as if she hadn't intended to bring God into the conversation. Probably in her line of work, discussing religion wasn't acceptable. He didn't care. In fact, talk of Jesus put him in mind of the Emily he'd known.

His lips curved. "Saint Emily."

Memory sparked in her eyes. "I apologize. Again. Bringing up my faith was inappropriate given the circumstances. I don't know what's wrong with me. I promise I am not usually so out of control. You seem to bring out the worst in me."

"I wonder why that is," he said softly.

Her shoulder lifted in a shrug that ended in a slump of despair. "Oh, Levi. What a sad, tragic mess."

Fighting the urge to take her in his arms and promise her anything she wanted, he crossed to where she sat and lowered himself to the cushion next to her. Gently, he lifted the sleeping baby from her lap onto his much longer thighs. Mason, warm as toast, snuggled right in.

Emily's thigh brushed his, and Levi knew right then

he'd never get over her, no matter how far he roamed. But to do what he thought was right, what was best for him as well as Mason, he'd have to disappoint her. Again.

Emily was lost to him anyway. Mason wasn't.

He swallowed the lump of sorrow. "Tell me what to do to become his legal guardian."

She was silent long enough to remind him that he was not her choice and that she disagreed vehemently.

"Are you absolutely sure?"

He was scared out of his mind, but the other options promised more regrets. He already had plenty of those, including the woman sitting next to him. "Yes."

"If you had to keep him by yourself for one full day, would you know what to feed him? How much? How often? Would you know if he was sick?" She pivoted in his direction. Their knees bumped. "Child care is a huge learning curve. Are you up for it?"

He was shaking in his boots. "Can't be that hard. People have babies all the time."

She rolled her eyes so far back in her head, they disappeared. "Which is why my case load gets heavier every day. Too many people having babies without knowing anything about proper parenting."

"I want to learn, Emily. Teach me." Gently, with emotion thick in his chest, he stroked the back of Mason's head. This little baby already had his heart. Might as well make it official. "I'll never be as good as his daddy, but I'll be the best uncle I can."

She did the silent thing again, and when he wondered if she would grab the baby and run, Emily took a deep breath and said, "There's paperwork involved. You'll have to undergo a background check and home study."

"Let's do it."

"The state also requires you to take classes."

His eyebrows came together. "He can't move in with me right away?"

"Not until the background check is cleared."

More delays. This could put a crimp in his plans to sell out and get moving.

"I'm not a criminal, Em, and I'd never do anything to hurt him. Look at him. He's so little." A single glance at the little man turned him to pudding.

"Standard procedure. Everyone has to have one."

"How long?"

"A few weeks, maybe six or thereabouts."

He'd be stuck here in Calypso for six weeks! Would Jack hold the manager's position for him? He'd have to ask and hope the man understood the importance of what he was about to do.

And if he didn't?

Levi would cross that bridge when he came to it. For now, he knew one thing for certain. Six weeks or six years. It didn't matter. He and Mason were going to be together.

"Is there any way to speed things up? I'm thinking about heading to Texas. Got a good job waiting for me."

"Texas?" The color drained from her face.

"Is it against the law to take him to Texas?"

"No, of course not. Once you're his guardian, where you live is your business."

He'd expected her to be thrilled that he would be out

of her sight, but she looked anything but pleased at his news.

He glanced down at the sleeping baby. "Meantime, he's stuck in foster care?"

Her nostrils flared. "I don't call being with me and Connie *stuck.*"

Levi leaned back and pinched the bridge of his nose. No matter what he said, she took offense. If he didn't know he owed her, he might get plum aggravated.

"I didn't mean that personally, Em." He pulled in a determined breath. "Tell me what to do, and I'll do it."

TEXAS? He was moving Mason to Texas?

She'd expected him to leave again, but not this soon. Not before she'd had a chance to be sure he'd take good care of the baby. Not before she came to grips with this crazy feeling she got every time she saw him.

Her eyes fell shut.

There was the crux of the matter. She was concerned for Mason, of course, but Levi's sincerity was undeniable. When he held Mason, his tender expression said it all. He would do his best.

The problem wasn't Mason or Levi's guardianship. The problem was in her heart.

He'd called her Em, as if they were still close, as if they still could be.

Hearing the nickname, the name he'd whispered in her ear so many times, did funny things to her insides. For a fraction of a second, she'd wondered what might happen between them if he stuck around. If they could be friends again.

And then, he'd dropped the bombshell. He was leaving. Again.

Levi, oh Levi. What are you doing to me?

Troubled, heavy-hearted, she guided him through the proper forms and showed him where to sign. Careful of Mason sleeping on his knees, he leaned the papers on the couch arm and scribbled his name. Though Emily had plenty of misgivings, Pastor Marcus had been proven right. Her feelings for Levi had gotten in the way. She'd considered them dead and gone, but being near him still made her skin tingle, her pulse beat a little faster. Made her remember what he'd done.

Looking back was futile. The past hurt too much, and there could be no future.

She gathered the papers and files, preparing to leave. As she reached for Mason, Levi put a hand on the baby's back.

"I'll carry him."

Gently, he lifted the ragdoll baby, attention riveted to the child. Something shifted in Emily, feelings she didn't want.

It was these feelings throwing her out of kilter.

Levi's hands looked huge against Mason's tiny form, huge and tender and cowboy manly. He slowly pulled the infant to his chest and patted Mason's tiny bottom. Another piece of ice chipped from around her heart.

Emily tried to look away and couldn't. "I have another home visit to make before church, Levi. I have to go."

"When can I see him again?"

"That's up to you."

"Can you bring him every day? If I'm going to learn..." He let the words dwindle. She knew what he meant. In her role as social worker, it was her place to teach him everything she could. While he was here.

"I'll try. If I don't have time, you can visit him at the Triple C. He'll be with Connie when I can't take him with me."

His lips curved and drew attention to his mouth. What would it be like to kiss him again? Would he still make her feel fragile and cherished the way he had before?

"Is Connie still the Triple C's head boss and the best cook in the county?"

His voice jerked her thoughts back to the present.

"That's Connie."

"They doing okay? Connie and Gilbert and your brothers?"

"Good. Real good. Gilbert has to watch his sugar these days—that Native American genetic thing—and Connie fusses over him."

"Connie fusses over everyone. Or she used to."

"Still does. If you need prayer or an enchilada or a helping hand, call Connie." The Donley boys had been the recipient of all three during their growing up years. "Nate married a great girl and Ace—well, Ace has his struggles, but he's still my brother, and I adore him."

"What about Wyatt?"

"Wyatt's a military man these days, the only brother without horse hay in his veins." And she worried about him more than she cared to admit.

"You're lucky."

"No, I'm blessed. Thankful, too, to have such a great family." Something Levi never had. And the truth of that softened her even more. He was never a bad boy. Mostly, he was a lonely, hurting teen who made the best of a bad situation. Would he do the same with Mason? Was it actually possible they could thrive together?

"You'll let Connie know I might stop in?"

"I'll leave the ranch phone number for you, but yes, you know Connie. She hasn't changed."

A wry chuckle left him. "Your dad was the one who gave me the long eye."

"That's because he was afraid you'd steal his little girl." She didn't know why she'd said that. Reminiscing wasn't good for either of them.

"You don't wear a wedding ring."

She jerked. Physically jerked. "My husband died in an oilfield fire six years ago."

"Em." His voice was breathy, shocked. "That's awful."

"One of the worst times of my life. Without the Lord —" Another reminder that only God could heal the pain of loss. Hers and Levi's.

His quiet gaze lingered on her face, and she could read the sympathy he struggled to express. He wanted to hold her. She could see it, always could. As a teen, she'd take the initiative, lean close and let those strong cowboy arms offer comfort.

As an older, wiser adult, she couldn't succumb to such foolish emotions. Especially now.

"Kids?" he asked kindly, taking one step closer.

"No." This was getting too personal, and she was

tumbling back in time so fast her vision was blurry. She had to snap out of it before she said or did something stupid. "I have to go, Levi."

This time she stood and reached down for Mason. Levi rose, too, standing so near she saw the flecks of green in his brown eyes and the thick spiky lashes surrounding them. They'd always said their babies would have beautiful eyes.

Swallowing the unexpected gulp of longing, Emily buckled Mason into his car seat and tried to understand the unwelcome surge of memories and emotions.

Maybe she wasn't over Levi Donley after all.

7

Friday morning the spring skies opened again and rain fell in a slow, steady stream. A dreary, depressing day that did nothing to ease Levi's grief. Much as he didn't like thinking about it, the clouds, the darkness, the steady rain brought to mind the flood that had taken his brother.

From his spot at the cheerful kitchen table, he gazed at the downpour and wondered if Choctaw Creek would overflow again. He worried that Emily might try to drive her SUV through the water.

She wouldn't, surely, but as he finished his scrambled eggs, he worried anyway.

The other night, he'd thought about kissing her. A selfish, inconsiderate thought on his part. She didn't need that kind of complication in her life.

He stuffed the last bite of toast into his mouth and pondered the problem of Emily. She was back in his life, whether by choice or by chance, and on his mind a lot.

He liked seeing her, liked getting to know her again. She'd always been special. The problem of Emily was not her. It was him. His father. His shame. His failure.

His cell phone buzzed, and when he saw the caller ID, Levi winced. Jack Parnell on The Long Spur. Another worrisome situation.

He pushed his plate to one side and answered. "Hey, Jack."

"Levi. I'm just checking in to see how things are going."

"It's been a rough couple of weeks, but I'm dealing. The realtor was due out here today for an appraisal, but it's raining again."

There was a short pause before Jack said, "You're in a tough spot, and I'm real sorry, but my current manager wants to leave at the end of the month. I was hoping to have you here before then." Jack was growing impatient. Levi could hear it in his voice. "Do you still want this position, or are you thinking of staying on there?"

Levi ran a hand over the back of his neck and squeezed at the tension building. "I want it, Jack. Managing a spread like yours is a dream job."

He'd waited years for a chance like this one.

"Can I expect you by the end of the month?"

Levi drew in a breath and let it out slowly. Jack wasn't going to like his answer.

"There's been a holdup on my nephew's guardianship, and the ranch needs some repairs before I put it on the market."

"How long are we talking about? I'm convinced you're the right man, but I can't hold this position indefinitely."

"I understand that, sir. Right now, since my brother's death, things are a little crazy. Hopefully, in a few weeks... maybe six at most."

The silence on the other end was not a good sign.

Finally, Jack muttered, "Call me at the end of next week, and let me know where you are," and hung up.

After staring at the dead phone for too long, Levi made another pot of coffee and moped around the kitchen, waiting, pondering. Would Jack hold the position? Or was the man even now looking for another ranch manager, one who could start right away, one who wouldn't come with the extra burden of an infant?

Rain pattered against the window panes, cold and relentless, like Jack's tone.

The manager's position on The Long Spur came with a house, benefits, a company truck, and a decent salary. None of the hassles of ownership and all the pleasure of ranching. A job like that was every cowboy's dream. If he could ever get there.

If Jack withdrew his offer, what then?

Levi had been sure he'd have everything settled by now, and yet, with each day another roadblock appeared. First, Mason and his paperwork. Then, the ranch issues and a herd of cows that needed attention. Now, the rain.

The lousy rain that had started everything.

Without doing the repairs, the ranch wouldn't bring top dollar, and Scott had worked too long and hard and put up with too much from their old man not to expect top dollar for his boy. A nice nest egg for Mason's future. With the sale, Scott's son could attend college if he wanted to, something his daddy had yearned to do.

Levi was determined Mason would enjoy everything he and Scott had missed out on.

But that meant spending time and money on the ranch now. Culling cows. Separating calves to brand or sell. Rebuilding fence. Fixing the water gaps. Retooling the water well. And so much more.

All the things he should be doing in Texas on The Long Spur.

Slipping into the full-length slicker that had carried him through many miles of bad weather, he braved the rain to do chores. Freckles met him in the barn eager to work.

"Only a short ride today, pal. A couple of springing heifers to move to the barn, and we'll call it done until the rain lets up."

His father would turn over in his grave if he heard those words. Slim never let any kind of weather keep him from sending his sons out to do chores.

Levi mounted up, hat down tight and collar flipped high. He rode out, crossing the pasture at an angle. He'd seen the cows near the back forty last night and now wished he'd brought them closer to the barn.

As they approached the far fence line, he caught sight of a neighboring homestead. Smoke curled from the chimney, warm and inviting.

With rain dripping from his hat, he scanned the ranch and wondered about the neighbors he had yet to meet. Maybe he never would.

At that moment, a small figure in an oversized hoodie appeared toting two five gallon buckets. A child. From the bend of her slender shoulders and her slow gait, the pails were full and heavy.

Levi nudged Freckles closer to the fence, dismounted, and climbed over the five strands of barbed wire.

"Hey there, need some help?" he called, taking long strides in the child's direction.

The young girl whirled, and the buckets sloshed.

He reached her side and gazed down at the forlorn little figure. She was maybe nine or ten. Slight of build. Too small to carry two five gallon buckets of what appeared to be hog feed.

Beneath the hoodie, blond hair stuck to a pale forehead. All of her was soaked through.

"Didn't mean to scare you." He reached for the buckets. "Let me carry those."

She shook her head, eyes widening. "I can do it. You shouldn't come over here. Daddy don't like people coming on our place."

"That a fact?" He took the buckets anyway. "Where to?"

"No, really, Mister. I can do it. Daddy will get mad."

"Is he in the house?"

She nodded. "Having breakfast."

Levi's jaw tightened.

He lifted the buckets and started toward the barn.

The little girl hissed. "No, please."

Raindrops dripped off her lashes and slid down her pale cheeks like tears. He knew the cold wrath of a harsh father. Was that her worry? He didn't want to cause trouble. It was bad enough she was out here in the pouring rain while her old man sat in a warm house stuffing his gut.

Reluctantly, knowing he could go no farther without upsetting the little girl, he left the buckets near the back of the barn, touched his fingertips to the brim of his drippy hat, and headed back to the patiently waiting Freckles.

He'd never met his neighbor, and already he wanted to punch the guy.

AROUND TEN, long after the heifers were settled in stalls and Levi had mended some tack and re-organized the tack and feed rooms, a big ranch truck rumbled down the long driveway.

When a sturdy, muscled cowboy in a gray Stetson stepped out into the rain, Levi opened the front door. Even after all this time, he recognized Emily's brother, Nate Caldwell.

What was he doing here?

He and Nate had been friendly, mostly because of Emily, and the two men had spent a couple of summers working side by side on the Triple C. Nate was a good guy. Or he had been.

Had Emily sent him? Was he here to convince Levi that moving on down the road was the best choice he could make? Without Mason?

Levi braced for it.

The other rancher wiped his boots on the *Bless all who enter* welcome mat and stepped through the door

Levi held open, toting a long dish of some kind. "Levi. Long time."

"How are you, Nate?"

Somehow they managed a handshake around the covered dish.

"That's what I came to ask you." Nate thrust out the dish. "Connie sent this over. Enchilada casserole."

Touched, Levi accepted the food. The spice-and-cheese scent rising from the still warm dish tantalized his taste buds.

"Tell her thanks. Smells great." The Triple C housekeeper was the first and only to send what locals termed funeral food, even if she was a week late. "Want some coffee? The rain is cold."

"Sure, if you have some ready."

"Not much else to do on a day like this."

"I hear ya." A raindrop toppled from Nate's hat brim to his brown shirt, leaving a dark spot. "I've got calves to separate and work, but they'll wait. The rain is supposed to move out tonight."

"Scott's cows should be nearly finished calving, too, but I haven't had a chance to read through all his records yet. Maybe tonight." The longer Levi stayed in Calypso, the more there was to do. And staying much longer was not an option. Not if Jack Parnell was to be his boss.

He motioned to the off-white couch. The checkered throw was rumpled and crooked, but a cowboy wouldn't care. "Sit. I'll put this in the kitchen and grab some coffee."

Levi carried the casserole to the kitchen and returned with two steaming mugs. He was on his sixth cup. As an old bunkhouse buddy used to say, he'd be able to thread a needle with the sewing machine running if he drank much more. But on a day like this, hot coffee hit the spot.

Surrounded on either side by Jessica's cheerful blue throw pillows, Nate took the mug and sipped. "Sorry I didn't get over here before now. Emily thought you might need some time."

Emily. Now they were getting to the topic Nate had probably come to discuss.

"It's been a tough week."

"Anything we can do?"

Levi studied the top of his coffee mug, heavy with the decisions he didn't know how to make. "Truth is, I don't even know."

"Are you open to ideas? Not pushing, just being neighborly."

His offer lifted Levi's dark mood a little. Nate hadn't come about Mason. He'd come as a friend. "Sure. Anything."

Nate leaned forward, elbows on his thighs, the coffee cup bracketed in his hands. Rough, rancher's hands, like Levi's.

"This is a good-sized ranch to work by yourself. Scott and I used to share the load fairly often. Don't be afraid to ask for help if you need it." He hitched his chin toward the south. "My hands and I helped him build that new hay barn. When our place nearly burned last fall, he was right there helping out for days. Watching flare ups, mending fence, checking cows, whatever needed doing."

"That was Scott."

"Yeah. Good man. Good neighbor and friend. Gonna be missed."

Levi blinked away the grief that rose in his chest, threatening to pull him under.

"I appreciate that, Nate. Knowing my brother mattered. It helps."

Had anyone ever said Levi mattered? Had he ever left a positive mark on people? He didn't think so, and the truth saddened him. He'd always been a rootless drifter, a man who didn't matter.

For Mason's sake, he'd have to settle down once and for all. Somewhere else. Preferably Texas.

"Scott mattered a lot, Levi," Nate said. "To folks like me who called him friend. To the church and community. You should have seen him working on that new annex building at Evangel Church. He would have everyone laughing even while we sweltered in the sun with a hammer and roofing shingles."

Levi nodded, heart tender for his brother. "He did that with me too. Dad would be working our tails off, and Scott would find a reason to joke around and make it fun. Feels good hearing he was happy."

"Crazy happy. Once he met Jessica, he was a different guy. They had something special." Nate's expression softened. "Like Whitney and me."

Levi jacked an eyebrow. "Emily mentioned a recent wedding."

The other cowboy's face glowed with pleasure. "Real recent. Right before Easter."

Easter. When Jessica and Scott were still alive. "So you're a newlywed. Congratulations."

Emily had been married at one time. Had she been happy? Had the lucky man been good to her? Had he realized what a treasure he'd found? Nate would know, and Levi wanted to ask. Wanted to but he didn't. No use stirring up the past.

"I'm a blessed man to have found a woman like Whitney and her little girls," Nate was saying, a slight smile curving his mouth.

Nate was a daddy. And Levi was about to be. His thoughts shot to his orphaned nephew. "Twins, I hear."

"Yep. Cutest things. Olivia and Sophia. They're three now." The rugged rancher lifted a pinky. "Got everyone on the Triple C wrapped right around here. One on each hand. Besides Jesus and Whitney, they're the best thing that ever happened to this old cowboy."

Levi sipped his coffee and let the warmth float over his tonsils and down in his belly. *Twins.* Quite an undertaking. He didn't know what he'd do if Scott had left him twins.

On second thought, he probably did know. Most likely, he would have headed to Texas as fast as his truck could haul.

And wasn't he pathetic?

But he was several days into the visitations with Mason and, though he was as awkward as a one-legged goose, he loved holding the little man. Loved when Mason opened those innocent eyes and cooed as if had something he needed to tell his Uncle Levi.

Uncle Levi. The title sat pretty easy even though the idea of being responsible for another human being for the rest of his life shook Levi worse than a tornado tearing through the front yard.

Some mornings he woke up with the strong temptation to hop in his truck and drive until he ran out of gas. Then Emily showed up in that orange car of hers with Mason in the back, and Levi was stuck like Gorilla Glue. Enamored. Besotted. Determined to be the daddy Scott couldn't be.

Which made him one messed up cowboy.

Nate set his cup on an end table. "Emily says you're thinking of moving to Texas."

Emily again.

"Got a job offer near Amarillo that I've wanted for a while. Ranch manager. I'll be selling this place and heading out there as soon as I can."

"The Donley Ranch is nothing to sneeze at, Levi. Scott saw to that." Nate studied him with serious eyes. "You'd be manager *and* owner if you stuck around here. Owner of a fine spread."

The man had no idea what he was saying. "No. Not here."

Nate fiddled with his coffee cup. His gaze shifted away and then returned. "Does your decision have anything to do with my sister?"

"No." *Yes.* "High school was ages ago. She's had a husband since then."

"No one forgets their first love."

Including him. Ten minutes with Emily and the truth had smacked him upside the head like a runaway two-by-four. "I think Emily has."

Nate gave him a long, considering look. "Back then, she would have followed you anywhere."

"I was no good for her."

Nate chuckled. "My dad would have agreed with your assessment."

"And you?"

"I thought you were a match made in heaven. So did Connie. Then you disappeared. Emily was devastated."

The words stabbed Levi in the gut. He'd hurt her. She'd suffered because of him. More reason than ever to stay away from her now.

"Long time ago, Nate, and one more reason for me to sell out. She doesn't need the reminders." Of things I can't share with you. Things I don't want to remember myself.

"She's not a kid anymore, Levi. She's strong and smart, and if she still cares for you, you're a lucky man."

Levi stared into his nearly empty cup. "She tolerates me. She's made that clear. She tolerates me for Mason's sake. She thinks I should give him up for adoption."

There. He'd blurted out his resentment, though Emily had every reason to consider him unfit as a parent.

"What do you think? Is that what Scott would have wanted?"

"No."

"There you go, then. Stick around. Raise that boy near people who loved his parents. Come home, Levi."

Home. Had this ranch ever been his home? Had he ever known a place he could call home?

Levi rubbed a hand over the back of his neck. "I don't know."

"A lot has changed around Calypso County and the

Donley Ranch. You might be surprised at how content you could be. Scott was."

He heard what Nate was too polite to say. Everyone in Calypso knew the Donley brothers didn't have the best home life, though none knew about the final straw that had broken the camel's back.

He did not, however, want to talk about his childhood. Never had. Wouldn't start today. Airing family problems simply wasn't done. Not by Donleys.

"Glad to hear it, but this town is not for me. I'm due in Texas by the end of the month."

Nate took another sip of his coffee, and the room was quiet while a wall clock ticked and rain pelted the windows and porch.

Nate seemed to have something else on his mind, so Levi sipped his java and waited him out.

"Your call, of course, but we'll be praying for the best outcome. For you *and* for Mason."

He wasn't used to people getting close enough to care, but at the mention of prayer, something cold inside Levi began to thaw. Emily used to pray about everything. Did she still? Had she prayed about him? About Mason? "I'm his uncle. He belongs with me."

"You're determined to raise him yourself?"

"I am." Funny how the more he said it, the more sure he was.

"Just remember, here in Calypso, you've got neighbors willing to lend a hand and a church that loved Mason and his parents." The other cowboy grinned. "And Connie would be ecstatic if you'd let her play grandma. You're in a tough spot, but you're not alone."

Something powerful and unfamiliar filled Levi's chest. He'd chosen to be alone for fourteen years. Raising Mason among caring friends would have advantages.

"If the rain holds off, I could use another hand to work calves on Tuesday." Fact was, he could use a whole bunkhouse full of cowboys for about a month to get this place whipped into top shape. But he wasn't ready to ask for that much help. Not unless his back was up against the wall. Nate had his own ranch to run.

Nate tipped his chin in acquiescence. "Give me a call when you're ready." Then he put down the now empty coffee cup and glanced toward the window. "Rain is slacking off. I'm headed to the feed store while I can. Welcome to come along if you'd like. Or drop by the Triple C any evening around six. Let Connie feed you and boss you around. Mostly in Spanish."

Nate's voice was full of affection. Levi remembered the Triple C housekeeper fondly, too. Connie been a mother figure to the Caldwell boys, a relationship Levi had envied.

"I'm headed over to the Triple C to visit Mason now." One less mile in rainy weather for Emily to drive.

"Think about what I said?"

"I will."

With a nod, Nate left the house, dashing through the rain, one hand holding his cowboy hat in place.

Levi watched from the doorway as his neighbor pulled away, big tires splashing through the driveway puddles.

Apparently, Nate held no grudge against for Levi for the wrong he'd done to Emily. He might if he knew the whole story, but for today, his old friend had given him food for thought.

At the word *food*, Levi's belly growled and suddenly he was hungry, really hungry, for the first time since his arrival. The spicy smell of Connie's casserole had something to do with the sudden return of his appetite, but it was more than that. It was Nate himself. The visit. The kind offer of friendship when he could have rightly punched Levi in the nose. It was what he deserved.

Nate Caldwell was a reminder that not every experience in Calypso been negative. It was also a rather stunning realization that he was no longer alone.

EMILY LEFT the rundown house with a heavy heart and three children in the backseat of her new SUV. The single mother had been so high on meth she hadn't even protested the removal of her kids, all under the age of eight. The children cried all the way to the foster family in the next town. Emily cried and prayed all the way back to the Triple C.

The rain and the dark brooding skies didn't help one bit.

"No matter how many times I have to remove kids from a home, it still tears me up," she told Connie when she stopped in for lunch and to see Mason.

"I know, *mija*. You have such a hard job." Connie offered her a sympathetic look and a glass of tea. "I will finish lunch. You go see Mason. He will cheer you."

Connie was right. Emily was head over heels in love with the tiny boy. Lunches on the run had become lunch at the Triple C and time with Mason. Evenings at community and church meetings now included Mason in her arms.

Letting him go would be harder than she'd expected, and she'd known from the start it wouldn't be easy. Letting him go to Levi would be even harder. Not that he wouldn't be good to the baby, but if he sold the ranch and took off to some distant state, she would never see Mason again.

Or Levi either.

All she could do was pray. The problem was, her prayers were a jumble. Prayers for Mason. Prayers for Levi. Prayers for herself not to fall for the rambling cowboy all over again. She'd thought she was immune. She'd been in love with Dennis. She'd been happily married for two whole years. But every time she talked to Levi or watched his awkward, heartfelt interaction with Mason, she softened a little more.

She had to hand it to the cowboy. He was trying hard to be the perfect uncle. And if the old dreams and plans they'd made together kept coming back in waves, she couldn't help it.

Had she judged him too harshly? Was she letting the past affect the present? Had she really, truly forgiven him?

In the upstairs bedroom—her old room—where the portable crib had been set up, she kissed the sleeping boy and smiled as he stretched in response. His eyes popped open, and he lay still, trying to focus. When he finally found her face, his tiny fists came up, and he flailed and kicked in excitement.

He recognized her voice, her face. She, in turn, recognized his moods and was learning his different cries.

She sighed, aware she had overstepped the bounds of professional duty and had set herself up for heartache. Mason was her temporary ward, not her child, and she would do well to remember the line between business and personal pleasure.

But how did anyone who loved children remain objective about the innocent, precious baby of her best friend?

After a quick diaper change, she washed her hands and carried him into the dining room. "Look what I found, Connie. Wide awake and wet as the outdoors."

Connie stood at the bar tossing a spring salad decorated with red, ripe strawberries. "He is a charmer, that one. You eat. I will hold the baby."

"That's okay. I enjoy holding him." While she could. As long as she could.

Emily slid onto a tall bar stool and cradled Mason over one shoulder while she shook out a napkin one-handed.

Connie took the stool next to her, chattering sweet noises at Mason. The baby flailed his arms, eyes wide and shining.

Emily stabbed a strawberry and held it up. "Did these come from your garden?"

"*Si.* Good, no?"

"Delicious." She popped it into her mouth and let the tart sweetness burst on her tongue. "Mmmm. So good."

They were halfway through their meal when the doorbell chimed.

Connie pushed her plate aside. "Eat. I will get the door."

Emily stabbed a blueberry and a bite of romaine and swirled her fork around in the homemade vinaigrette. Connie could make anything taste delicious. Even lettuce.

She heard voices coming toward the kitchen. Connie's and that of a man, a quietly drawling baritone. Emily's heart jumped. Was that Levi?

She finished chewing, dabbed her mouth with a napkin and twisted the stool around. Mason nuzzled her neck and cooed. Breathing in his baby scent, she waited.

Hat in hand, Levi followed Connie into the dining room. His eyes locked onto hers and, faster than a wink, Emily was lost. In dark jeans and a button-down shirt, Levi had dressed up, the way he used to when he'd come to pick her up and take her out somewhere. The movies. A ballgame. Fishing in one the Triple C's many ponds. So many places they'd enjoyed together, places when he could sneak way from his slave-driving father.

Levi paused. "Sorry to interrupt your lunch. I didn't think about the time. Connie said I could come whenever."

"I'm finished." She couldn't take another bite. Not with six feet of handsome cowboy making her remember a better time.

"Emily." Connie cleared her throat. "Levi came to visit Mason."

Emily blinked, embarrassed. What was wrong with her? Levi wasn't here to see her. They weren't kids any longer.

"Of course." She laughed self-consciously and fluttered a hand toward the baby. "I had planned to bring him to see you tonight."

"My roads are real muddy." He stood uncomfortably next to her chair, one finger stroking Mason's arm. "I didn't want you to get stuck in that fancy new car of yours."

The gesture touched her. Levi had always been thoughtful that way. If he could make her life easier, he did. She'd forgotten about that.

"You want to hold him?"

He showed her his hands and smiled. Sun crinkles built spokes around his brown eyes. "I washed up before I came."

As if she hadn't noticed.

She returned the smile and stood up from the bar to make the baby exchange. He smelled like shave lotion and rain. "He'll be hungry soon. I'll fix a bottle. You can sit here if you want."

"I think," Connie said, "the living room would be more comfortable, Levi. Go." She shooed him with both hands. "I will bring a shoulder pad."

"Shoulder pad?" Emily heard him ask as he accompanied Connie into the next room. "I don't think he's ready for football."

She snickered at the silly statement but quickly sobered. Didn't his lack of experience with babies prove that Mason would be better off with someone fully prepared to take on the responsibility?

Maybe. She wasn't as sure about that anymore. And if

she was truthful, her worry was more selfish than she wanted to admit.

From the living room came the sound of Levi's warm baritone and Mason's responding coos and gurgles. Endearing. Precious.

She bit her lip, facing the real issue at hand.

As long as Levi remained right here in Calypso, everything would work out fine. If he and the baby were nearby, she could keep an eye on things.

Yes, everything would be fine.

If she could manage to keep her heart under control.

8

L evi spruced up the living room, ran a dust rag over the coffee table, and put on a fresh pot of coffee. Emily was due any minute. With Mason.

After his latest visit to the Triple C, Emily had changed. Maybe he'd somehow proved himself worthy of caring for Mason. Or maybe she'd realized she couldn't win and tossed in the towel. Either way, she now seemed almost agreeable to the idea of his adopting the boy. Anyway, she didn't constantly nag him to change his mind.

In the days since, they'd fallen into a regular routine. Nearly every day, Emily shot him a text and brought Mason to the ranch. Sometimes she appeared in the afternoon but usually after her regular work hours ended. If the evening extended longer each time, he wasn't complaining.

Rubbing at his almost healed knee, Levi considered an ice pack, but there wasn't time. He didn't want Emily thinking he was too banged up to raise Mason. She already had enough reservations in that department.

During the day, he worked his body until he was nearly crippled trying to get the ranch ready to sell. Jack Parnell had called with the news that, given the tragic circumstances, the retiring manager had agreed to stay on a few weeks longer.

At least, he had some breathing room.

Time to become a daddy. Time to fix the ranch. Time to make his brother proud. Time to prove his worth to Emily.

He stashed the dust rag under the kitchen cabinet and sniffed the air. Lemon cleaner. Cooking smells. No cow manure.

He checked his boots. All good.

Even though Mason technically qualified as part of Emily's job, Levi liked to think she enjoyed being here. With him. At least they were talking, and often they shared a laugh and reminisced about the good times, though he avoided anything that even resembled a discussion of the event that had driven them apart.

Good times. There *had* been some of those. Being with Emily not only brought back the humiliation and regret, it forced him to examine his time here and the time in between.

His anger and resentment toward his father had affected every decision he'd ever made. Maybe it was time to do something about that.

Emily must be praying for him. He was doing a little of that himself. Thinking about God. Praying. He'd even found Scott's Bible and read a few of the red parts.

But the resentment toward the old man still festered like a wound left untreated.

He and Emily were such different people now. He was the problem. She was pretty special, as always. Educated, successful, and in high demand, Emily was a Calypso powerhouse whose magpie of a cell phone chirped constantly. People liked her, needed her expertise, wanted her on committees. Someone even asked her to run for mayor. She'd turned that request down flat and laughed after she'd hung up.

He'd laughed with her, feeling good, feeling positive. He'd teasingly referred to her as, "Mayor Em."

Teenage Emily had been beautiful, warm, and generous. The adult Emily was all those things, but she was more. Much more.

He already knew what she thought of the adult Levi. Drifter, irresponsible. He couldn't argue the point. He'd been all that. Still was, though he was trying to change.

Lately, he thought she liked him anyway.

He sure liked her.

His pulsed bucked like a wild bronco every time she texted him or turned down the lane to his house.

Like now, he was antsy, anxious, eager to see her and the miniature cowboy.

Yeah. He liked that idea. Mason would be a cowboy like his daddy. And his uncle.

He paced to the window to stare out. No sign of a burnt orange SUV. He went back to the kitchen and set out a plate of grapes to impress her with health food. Didn't want her thinking he didn't know how to properly feed a growing boy.

Not that Mason was anywhere near ready for solid food.

Yesterday she'd arrived in mid-afternoon because she attended church on Wednesday night. She'd even invited him to go along. He hadn't, but he'd thought about it. Nate had texted him an invite to a men's fellowship breakfast on Saturday, too. What would it hurt? If he was honest, he could use some extra prayers right now. The ranch repairs and Mason's paperwork were taking forever.

He couldn't put Jack Parnell and The Long Spur off much longer.

For the third time since coming in from the pasture, he washed and dried his hands. Babies were susceptible to germs. Emily never let him forget.

When a knock sounded, he rushed to the front door and yanked it open. His stomach dropped in disappointment.

The visitor wasn't Emily. She was much shorter and a lot younger—a slender little girl in jeans and T-shirt, maybe nine or ten, with long, cotton-pale hair and a scatter of light freckles across her cheekbones. She looked familiar.

"Who are you?" the girl asked with the frankness of childhood.

"Levi Donley. Who are you?"

"Daisy Beech." She turned and pointed across his pasture. "I live over there."

Ah, so that's who she was. "In my pasture?"

She giggled, one hand against her mouth. "No, silly, in

my dad's house on the other side of the fence. Besides, this isn't your pasture."

At the moment it was, but he didn't know how to explain the situation to a child.

"We've met before."

She tilted her pert face up and up, forehead scrunched in thought. Her nearly invisible eyebrows merged into one. "We have?"

"In the rain. I carried your buckets to the barn."

"That was *you?*" she asked as if he was a rock star or something.

"Yep. You didn't get in any trouble, did you?"

"No."

Maybe he'd misread the situation. He had a habit of projecting his bad experiences onto other situations. He certainly hoped for her sake he'd been mistaken.

Levi leaned out to scan the driveway for an orange SUV before returning his attention to the child. "What can I do for you, Daisy?"

"I came to see Mason. Miss Jessica let me hold him every single day." Her eyes grew glassy, and she sniffed. "She was my friend."

Levi felt a pinch of fire behind his nose and rubbed at it. "I hear she was a real nice lady."

Daisy's head bobbed. Her hair could use a comb. "She was. So was Mr. Scott. He let me ride his horse sometimes. And Miss Jessica took me to children's church. Sometimes she'd braid my hair, and she gave me these for my birthday." The little girl stuck out a foot encased in sparkly pink sneakers.

"I guess you heard about what happened." Levi hoped she had, so he wouldn't have to explain.

The bottom lip quivered, and the palest eyelashes imaginable fluttered up and down. She was fighting tears. Trying to be strong. Gutsy, he thought, for such a little thing.

"They died. Daddy wouldn't let me go to the funeral. I wanted to. But Mason didn't die, and I thought he would be home by now." Face sad, mouth downturned, she raised her palms in a shrug. "Where else would he be?"

"Babies can't live alone, Daisy." To cheer her, Levi widened his eyes and offered his silliest, most horrified look. "They can't cook."

The sunny giggle returned. "I know that. I thought he'd be here with *you*. This is his house."

In a manner of speaking, Daisy was right. This was Mason's home, his birthright. Was selling out the best choice for his nephew?

He didn't know, didn't want to think about it. He despised this ranch and was selling it, and that was that.

"Mason is with the social worker right now. She should be here any minute, if you want to hang around and see him."

Daisy clapped her hands together. "Oh, I do. I truly do. Thank you, Mister—" Her forehead scrunched again. "What did you say your name was?"

"Levi."

The rumble of a car engine spun them both toward the end of the driveway, where the main road ran east and west. The glint of burnt orange made Levi's heart leap.

And there went his rambunctious bronco pulse again.

Emily was here.

EMILY SAW HIM COMING, saw those long, jean-clad legs stride toward her car, saw a light in his eyes. Was it for her? Or the baby? Or was grief's grip finally loosening enough for him to breathe again?

A flutter of awareness, the one that started when she'd first talked to him after Jessica's funeral and wouldn't go away, danced in her belly. The past weeks of visits were getting under her skin. Seeing him so much, being in his company, watching him with Mason—all that and more was getting under her skin. The Levi she'd known was still there, but in the interim years, he'd become a stronger, more appealing man—if such a thing were possible.

Like her, he was falling hard for Mason. Sometimes he looked at her as if he might be falling for her, too.

This afternoon, Connie had fretted, afraid she was getting too involved with Levi, worried she'd get hurt again. Emily had denied it, of course, claiming Mason's best interest, but to herself, she couldn't deny the tumultuous emotions the cowboy stirred.

She wasn't a complete idiot. Levi had been very clear in his intentions. He was moving to Texas ASAP. Nothing in Calypso could hold him. Certainly not her.

She'd already loved two men who'd left her. She didn't want to go through that again.

Levi reached the car and pulled the handle to open

her door. Cowboy courtesy. He would open doors for any woman.

She stepped out, attention going to the blond child who had followed the cowboy to the car. "Oh. You have a visitor. Hello, Daisy."

"Hi, Miss Emily."

Levi looked surprised. "You two know each other?"

She saw the flare of wariness in the little girl's eyes and kept the explanation simple. "From church. Daisy and Jessica were very good friends."

"I came to see Mason." Daisy stuck her hands behind her back and rocked on sparkly blue tennis shoes. "Mr. Levi said I could."

"Of course, you can." Emily pivoted toward the back of the car, but Levi was already there unbuckling the carrier.

"Look at him." Levi motioned to the arm-flailing baby. "He wants me to pick him up. He's reaching for me."

Emily snorted. "He wants out of that car seat."

He shot her a slanted look. "Don't be a spoiler. He's flapping and kicking, and any minute, he'll grin like he did last time."

Mason *did* seem to respond to the cowboy, particularly to his voice, a good sign for bonding. The little one twisted his head to follow the sound, eyes wide open and staring.

Emily was tempted to do the same.

As if they weighed nothing, Levi hoisted the baby and carrier and led the parade into the house.

A man with a baby did funny things to a woman's heart. To *her* heart.

Unaware of her admiring stare, he deposited the carrier onto the couch. "Come to Uncle Levi." The cowboy lifted Mason from the car seat. "Whoa, little man, you're getting heavy. What is this woman feeding you? Bricks? Cars? Elephants?"

Daisy, bouncing like a trampoline, giggled. "You're funny."

Mason cooed as if in agreement.

Emily blinked. Levi? Funny? She remembered a serious boy with the load of the world on his shoulders.

Scott had been the joker. Levi had been the deep one, the boy who listened to her rant about the world's injustices and cheered her on in support of her many causes.

Once, he'd stayed up all night with her and a handful of others to pack shoeboxes for orphans in Africa and then worked on this very ranch all the next day in the heat and sun without so much as a nap. Slim Donley allowed no slacking.

She had never forgotten that kind and loving boy, a boy who didn't know how to express himself any way except through hard labor. Emily had been the expressive one, the one who'd reached out to him.

Now she was too afraid.

Hand over her rapidly beating heart, she took a seat on the couch next to him. His manly scent washed over her in more memories. Once upon a birthday, she'd given him cologne, and he'd been stunned and painfully grateful. His father didn't buy presents. Hers were the only birthday gifts Levi had ever received.

He'd worn the Cool Water every day until the bottle was empty. He wore that fragrance today.

Had he always worn the crisp, fresh scent? Or had he remembered and bought it again because of her? An impossible yearning for something long past tightened in her chest.

Daisy, clearly enamored of Mason, perched on the other side of Levi and jiggled the baby's hand.

"Ready to hold him?" Levi lifted one eyebrow toward the excited little girl.

Daisy's head bobbed up and down. "Miss Jessica showed me. I know how."

"Then you're way ahead of me. I'm still learning." With a reassuring wink, Levi placed the baby in the girl's outstretched arms.

Daisy stared down at Mason with the sweetest expression. Poor little kid. Harsh father. No mother. She'd been dealt a difficult lot in life.

Levi's lot hadn't been much different.

He met her eyes across the Daisy's pale blond head. "Want some coffee or tea?"

"Water is fine."

"I have grapes," he said hopefully.

Her lips curved. He always tried to feed her. "No cookies this time?"

He grinned right back. "A man doesn't give up his Oreos that easily. I'm thinking Daisy would like a few, too."

"How about it, Daisy?" Emily asked.

Daisy's blue eyes sparkled. "Miss Jessica gave me cookies sometimes. I *love* Oreos."

When Levi started toward the kitchen, the little girl called, "Don't bring any for Mason. He doesn't have any teeth."

"What?" Levi teased. "No teeth? How will he eat that T-bone steak I was gonna fix for supper?"

Daisy giggled and scrunched her shoulders. To Emily, she said, "He's nice. I like him. Don't you?"

Yes, she did. Very much. But *like* was as far as she would let things go.

She held a finger to her lips. "Don't tell him. His head will get too big for his hat."

"I heard that." Levi returned with the snacks and reclaimed Mason.

Emily watched with a full feeling in her chest as he cajoled smiles and coos from his nephew.

"Admit it. I'm getting good at this," he said to Emily with a smug look.

"Maybe," she conceded.

For all her misgivings, she was coming to realize that the cowboy could be a good parent to Mason.

She studied the man, his handsome face, the dimple in his chin that perfectly matched Mason's, the tenderness he displayed toward the baby and the little girl.

Oh, heart, what are you doing?

When he takes that baby and leaves, what will you do?

But he hadn't mentioned Texas or selling the ranch in days. Maybe he was growing fond of Calypso. Maybe he would stay.

Mason began to fuss and squirm. In seconds, he was in an all out, red-faced squall.

Daisy gently patted the infant's cheek. "Don't cry, baby. Don't cry."

Levi's confident air disappeared like Daisy's Oreos—

fast. With worried eyes, he looked at Emily. "What's wrong? Is he hungry?"

"Most likely. It's nearly seven."

"Seven?" Daisy's pale eyes widened. She jumped to her feet. "I have to go. Right now!"

In a flurry, she rushed to the door but spun around. Over Mason's cries, she asked, her face pinched and anxious, "Can I come back?"

Levi nodded. "Anytime."

Then she was gone, sparkly shoes pounding across the wooden porch.

"What was that all about?" Levi jiggled the crying baby.

Emily rummaged in the diaper bag for a bottle, unsure how much to share. She knew Daisy, knew about her home life, and was concerned. As a social worker, confidentiality was important, but on the other hand, Levi was a neighbor, and Daisy would be coming around. He could keep an eye out for trouble.

"Let's get him settled first, and then we'll talk."

With a small frown denting the space between his eyebrows, Levi followed her into the kitchen where she ran warm water over the bottle. She dried off the excess moisture and popped the nipple into Mason's open mouth. Silence descended. Total, abject silence.

"He sure can make a lot of noise," Levi said in awe.

Emily smiled tenderly at the little one. The way Mason stared up at Levi as if the cowboy had saved his life touched a tender spot inside.

"Wait until you're dead asleep and he starts wailing like that. He scares me right out of bed."

They were standing close. She should move away. Levi grinned down at her. She stayed right where she was.

"I'd like to see that."

"No, you wouldn't. Trust me. Wild hair sticking up everywhere, no make-up. Ugly."

"You're always beautiful, Emily. Nothing can change that." He'd gone as serious as a heart attack—like the one she was about to have. She really should step back. Or better yet, grab Mason and head for home. She didn't.

The air crackled with an emotion she'd never wanted to feel again. Levi felt it too. He swallowed and shifted his gaze from her to the baby and back again.

"Em," he started softly.

Em. The nickname that turned her to mush.

Calling on memories of a teenage girl crying her eyes out for weeks and weeks, and with the word *Texas* in her mind, Emily turned away.

"Let's move to the living room, shall we?"

THE WOMAN BEWILDERED HIM. But then, women always bewildered him. He wasn't a complete dunce, but she'd said she liked him. He'd thought maybe they were becoming close again.

No such luck.

With a sigh, he carried the slurping, smacking infant to the living room but chose the chair across from Emily instead of sitting next to her again.

She might like him a little, but she didn't want him to get too close.

"You wanted to know about Daisy." Emily was all business now, hands in her lap and back straight as a two-by-four. He'd upset her, but he didn't know how or why, nor did he know how to ask.

"She seems like a nice kid."

"She's a terrific little girl, and Jessica adored her, mentored her, and tried to be the mother figure Daisy doesn't have. Her mom died when Daisy was born."

The revelation hit him right in the sternum. His mom hadn't died. She'd left when he was four and Scott was two, but he understood growing up without a mother. "Poor kid."

"Yes, and to make matters worse, her dad is no candidate for father of the year."

Emily bent forward and plucked a grape from the plate but studied it instead of eating. "I'm limited on what I can say because of my job, but some things are common knowledge."

"I know a little." He told her about meeting Daisy in the rain. "She was scared her dad would see me. She said he didn't like strangers on his land."

"That's her father's right, of course, to limit visitors." She raised a palm. "I know. And I agree with you, but Arlo Beech is not the neighborly kind."

"Is he abusive?" Levi's shoulders tensed. "Does he hit her?"

If he did, Levi would cross the pasture and engage in a little man-to-man.

"No evidence of abuse at this point. She does miss a lot of school, which is where I come in." She rolled the grape between her thumb and index finger. "From my single encounter at their home, and by all accounts from her teachers and what Jessica told me, he's a difficult, demanding man. But there's no law against being a jerk, as you can attest."

He huffed, his jaw tightening. Could he ever. The old man hadn't been a beater, but he'd been every other kind of hard case. "Sad deal."

"I suspect the relationship is anything but warm and fuzzy. Daisy's a ray of sunshine, a born optimist, but she's needy too. She latched on to Jessica like a wood tick. According to Jessica, her dad doesn't like for her to leave the property, but she'd sneak across the field any time she could to be here."

"Where someone cared about her."

"That was Jessica's take, and mine too. She absolutely blossomed when Jessica began taking her to church."

Now her generous, caring mother figure was gone. "Does she have anyone else? Siblings maybe?"

"She's an only child."

Harsh, demanding father. No mother. He could definitely relate. At least, he and Scott had had each other.

He was getting a real bad attitude toward his neighbor across the back fence.

"She can hang out over here any time," he said gruffly. As long as he was here.

"Perhaps I could speak to her father and ask permission to take her to church the way Jessica did."

"That's a great idea," Levi said. "I remember how much the VBS meant to me and Scott. Being around kind people and learning that not all men were like my dad made a difference."

Mason squirmed and began to fuss, reminding Levi to tilt the bottle higher.

"Not to push," Emily said softly, "but Evangel Church still has some great people, many of whom you know. You should come."

"You're the second person today to invite me." He told her about Nate's text. "Must be a conspiracy."

"A Jesus conspiracy of love."

The word *love* took on a new meaning. She didn't speak of romantic love. He knew that. But he couldn't stop his thoughts from going there. Not that he had any right. No right. At. All.

Her face grew tender, and she tilted her chin toward the baby in his arms. "He needs to be burped."

A reprieve from a too-serious topic.

Mason squirmed, grunting as he fought against the half-empty bottle with his mouth. "Either that, or he's doing something diabolical to his diaper."

Emily laughed, a real laugh that warmed Levi from the inside out. "You get diaper duty if that's the case."

"I might as well get used to it. This little cowboy is stuck with me." He hadn't been there for Scott. He could be there for his son. "Any news on my background check?"

"We should hear soon. All the paperwork's been submitted." A frown appeared between her smooth, dark eyebrows. "Are you positive about this, Levi?"

He wasn't sure about a lot of things—his future, the ranch, and particularly, his strange feelings for Emily—but Mason? He had no doubt. "I won't let him down."

"Mason or Scott?"

"Both."

"You can't raise a child out of guilt."

They were back to that, the abandonment. Of her. Of Scott. Sure he had guilt, but guilt was not his motivation for wanting Mason.

He blew out a frustrated breath. "I get that you despise me, Emily, and I get why. But is it so hard for you to believe that I might care about him?"

"I don't despise you. I never did. I couldn't."

The quietly spoken words pierced his heart. Her pained expression shook him.

"Not even..." He glanced away from those soft green eyes and swallowed. *Do not go there.*

"We've never talked about what happened, Levi. Maybe we should clear the air once and for—"

"Don't. Leave it."

The last thing he needed was to rehash a day of humiliation and loss with reminders that he'd let her down, that he'd hurt her.

She didn't say any more, but her eyes darkened and grew glassy. An uncomfortable silence filled the room, leaving him with the feeling that he was exactly the sorry cowboy she thought he was.

Emily rifled in the diaper bag and, after a few painful moments, came at him with Mason's baby blanket. "We should go."

"Em—" He stuttered, searching for the words. He'd never been good at saying the right things. "Cut me some slack, okay? I'm trying."

Her face softened. She put a hand on his forearm. "I know. You'll do fine."

"I will. I promise." He gently held the baby away from his body, so she could wrap him in the blanket.

Mason stretched and made cute, groaning noises. Levi's gaze connected with Emily's. They both smiled, and a balloon of pleasure expanded in his chest.

"Every time you bring him out here, I wish you didn't have to leave."

"You mean, you wish Mason didn't have to leave."

He didn't want either of them to go. Every day Emily was here, he remembered more of the reasons he'd once loved her.

A very bad idea.

"I worry," she said.

"About me doing something stupid?"

She bit down on her lip and fiddled with the soft blue blanket. "Are you still taking the job in Texas?"

His heart jumped, both hopeful and dismayed. Did she want him here? Was that what she was trying to say? Could she possibly have forgiven him? "Why does it matter where I go?"

She put a hand on Mason's chest. "This is his home."

Levi's heart tumbled back to earth. Her concern was for Mason. Levi was not part of the equation. And he couldn't even argue with her logic.

9

The yellow dog showed up on the same day the black bull disappeared. A skinny shepherd-lab without a collar and so covered in fleas, Levi bathed him in a stock tank and then apologized with a pound of hamburger meat he'd bought for his own dinner. The dog had not left his side since.

The bull, however, was nowhere to be found, and good bulls were costly. This one was a registered Angus with a strong pedigree, low birth weight calves, and an amiable disposition. In other words, highly valuable.

After driving much of the property, Levi saddled Freckles to ride the fence lines and figure out how the bull, red tag number 1 with a cross-D brand, had escaped. The yellow dog trotted eagerly beside the horse. Levi was surprised he had the strength.

As they approached the back forty, Daisy's house came into view.

The little girl seemed to have radar for baby Mason.

She came running each time Emily drove into the yard. Out of breath and beaming as if she hadn't a care in the world, she would come to play with Mason. After an hour or so, she'd jet out the door and race across the field toward home, claiming "chores."

For a nine-year old, she was an independent little girl with a lot to do.

Emily had convinced Daisy's father to let her attend church, and Levi figured that was a good sign. So good that he'd started going too.

The thing was, the messages from the pulpit seemed directed at him as if the minister knew exactly what was on his mind. As if the shiny-eyed preacher knew the confusion and hurt and shame Levi had never been able to shake. As if he understood Levi's anger and resentment toward his old man.

Could Jesus help with all that garbage?

It was something to ponder, something to discuss with Emily.

With a squeeze of one leg against Freckles's belly, Levi turned the appaloosa along the fence line toward the only gate on this side of the property. The ground was soft in places, scented by moist earth and spring grass. Since he was here, he might as well get acquainted with Daisy's dad and ask if the other rancher had seen the lost bull.

He and his horse entered the property and, as he rounded the farmhouse and approached the front door, a man stepped out...with a rifle in hand.

As he'd halfway expected, not a warm welcome.

Levi tugged Freckles to a stop. The dog stopped next

to the horse and hunkered low, pinning the neighbor with a wary stare.

"Mr. Beech? I'm you're neighbor, Levi Donley."

"I know who you are. Scott Donley's brother." The twist of Beech's lips said he didn't care much for Scott. Had the pair butted heads?

"I took over the ranch after my brother's death." Saying the word *death* still choked him.

The man on the porch shifted, his stance not relaxing one bit. "I don't like my girl over there so much."

No condolences, no compassion.

Nice guy. "She's not bothering anyone."

"Bothers me. I don't much like that social worker either sticking her nose in our business. Like Donley's wife. Uppity."

"Daisy's a little girl. Maybe she needs a woman in her life."

The man spat. "Don't you think I know that? Only reason I let her go off to that holier-than-thou church. As long as she keeps up with her chores and doesn't come home preaching to me about God and all that nonsense."

A slow boil started in Levi's belly. He didn't like Arlo Beech at all. He reminded him too much of Slim Donley.

Holding back his temper and the words burning in his throat, Levi shifted in the saddle, leather creaking. From the corner of one eye, he caught a flash of red. Following the line of sight, his anger grew hotter.

He kept his tone intentionally calm. "That's my bull in your lot over there."

The rifle didn't move, but the man glanced down at the weapon. "How can you be so sure he's yours?"

"Black angus. Red ear-tag number one, and I'm willing to bet he's carrying the Donley brand."

"Possession is nine-tenths of the law."

Levi's jaw clenched and unclenched. "Stealing cattle is illegal."

"Didn't steal him. He just showed up. Can't blame a man for that. Nice bull. And I got cows." Beech grinned, though the expression was anything but friendly. "I guess he was lonely."

Several thoughts roamed through Levi's brain while Freckles, feeling his owner's tension, moved restlessly. Harness jingled. A slight breeze ruffled the new grass.

Levi patted the animal's neck and considered his options. He could get off this horse and punch the guy. Call the sheriff. Or get his bull and get out of here.

The last seemed the most prudent. For now.

Turning the gelding without further comment, he picked his way around the house to the barn and into the barn lot.

Freckles knew the drill. Together, they hazed the docile bull out of the pen slow and easy. Hurrying cattle was the quickest route to failure.

Levi could feel Beech watching, and the hair tingled on the back of his neck.

The yellow dog must have felt it too. He turned his scrawny body toward the house and growled low in his throat.

In the five-minute conversation, Levi had learned two things. He didn't like Arlo Beech one bit, and he was determined to watch out for Daisy.

EMILY HAD STALLED as long as she could. She'd put in a full day of work including a court appearance, a meeting with a child advocate, a child removal, and a pile of paperwork. Her time was up.

"Help me get through this, Jesus."

Fighting tears, she loaded Mason and his belongings into the back of her SUV and made the drive to the Donley Ranch.

The background clearance had arrived. The paperwork was complete. The state was satisfied that Mason's best interests had been served. The official court appearance would happen later, but tonight, Jessica's son would move in with Levi permanently. And Emily was one step closer to losing him, and Levi, forever.

A tear slid down her cheek. She gripped the steering wheel tighter.

Uniting children with their forever home was normally a joyous occasion. Usually, she was so thrilled for baby and parents than she bought balloons and a cake to celebrate the newly formed family.

Today the exchange cut like a knife. Not because she didn't trust Levi to take care of the child. She did. Though he had a lot to learn about baby care, he had done absolutely everything she'd suggested and more.

Levi wasn't the problem. Not completely. She was.

She loved Mason. As a woman who had put the idea of having children on the back burner, Jessica's baby had captured her heart and made her long to be a mother.

For a few short weeks, she *had* been a mother. And she'd loved it, sleepless nights, dirty diapers and all. If

Levi took the job in Texas as he planned, her heart would shatter in tiny pieces.

Another tear slipped loose.

There was the problem. Fear. Worry that Levi would leave and she'd never see Mason again. And maybe fear that she'd never see Levi again either.

She clicked on the radio to K-LOVE, her favorite Christian station, and tried to sing along. Mostly she prayed.

By the time she drove onto the Donley Ranch, she had her emotions under control.

"It's part of the job, Mason." She inhaled a long, calming breath and let it out. "We can do this."

Her spirits lifted slightly to see Daisy hopping up and down on the front porch like a human pogo stick. A whip-thin dog of questionable parentage watched her with open-mouthed pleasure as Levi exited the house wearing a grin on his face and a blue dish towel over one shoulder. He held up both hands as if to say, "clean."

In spite of her melancholy, Emily smiled. Clean hands had become a joke between them.

The man and the neighbor girl fell upon the car and began hauling in Mason's belongings from the back seat. The dog hung back, his tail moving slowly as if asking permission to approach.

"Whose dog?"

Levi shrugged. "A stray, I think. Starving."

"Poor thing. So skinny. Did you feed him?"

He frowned. "Wouldn't you?"

"He seems sweet. Are you going to keep him?"

Levi glanced away. "Depends."

Emily's stomach clenched. She pressed her lips together and glanced aside to get her act together before asking, "Are they still holding the job in Texas?"

"For now." He didn't look too happy with the question, and she wondered if he was afraid of losing the job, or if he was having second thoughts about leaving. Lord forgive her, she wished for either to happen.

Everything depended on whether or not he sold the ranch and moved on. Far away. This time, with Jessica's baby.

She pushed the remote button to open the rear of the SUV. More boxes and baby things were piled inside.

Levi fisted both hands on his hips, expression amazed. "He's got a lot of stuff for such a little guy."

Maybe she had a gone a little crazy buying things for him.

"You have no idea how quickly he goes through outfits." Especially since she changed him every couple of hours for the fun of it. Jessica had done the same.

"He has more clothes upstairs in the nursery," Levi said.

"Probably too small by now."

Levi's eyebrows drew together. "You think? Already?"

"Babies grow fast."

She handed Mason off to Daisy, who'd been dancing a circle around the cowboy. The child flashed a dazzling smile and carefully, slowly, carried Mason inside the house.

Emily grabbed the car seat while Levi toted a stack of boxes.

She stopped just inside the doorway to sniff the air. "Something smells delicious."

"Dinner." Levi's expression was uncertain. "I thought maybe...you might stay for supper."

She glanced toward Daisy and Mason. The little girl had put a blanket on the carpet and was lying next to Mason making him gurgle and grin. His tiny arms and legs pumped like mad. "Well, I—"

"For him, I mean," Levi rushed to say. "I'll need some more pointers before you go."

Right. For Mason. As it should be. With forced cheer, she asked, "What are we having?"

He held up a finger. "One moment."

Whipping the dish towel from his shoulder, he hurried into the kitchen, boots tapping against the tile. Emily followed. Daisy and Mason were having a blast without them.

Bent low over the oven, he said, "Baked fish sticks and Brussels sprouts."

"Oh. That sounds...nice." Actually, it sounded gross. She wasn't crazy about fish sticks, and she hated Brussels sprouts.

Levi flashed her a grin. "Kidding. How about chicken parmesan instead?"

Her favorite dish? He'd remembered?

A cold spot warmed. "You know how to make chicken parmesan?"

"Well..." His gaze grew shifty. "Got the recipe from the internet."

She laughed. "Should be interesting."

He hiked an eyebrow, a twinkle in his eyes. "Are you game?"

"How can I resist?" Even though she should.

Self-preservation told her to leave sooner rather than later, but, she told herself, Mason would need her. Tonight, he would sleep in a different bed and room, and Levi would require assistance to get him bathed and settled. If she wasn't here, who would sing his favorite lullaby?

She flashed a glance at the cowboy. He'd taken in a stray dog, a lonely neighbor child, an orphaned baby. Did he realize how kind and caring he was? And that he gave all the signals of putting down roots?

Who was she trying to fool? Mason wasn't the only reason she wanted to stay for dinner.

Flummoxed, needing to sort her thoughts, she pointed to the pile of baby items in the living room. "I'll go up and start putting things away."

Levi closed the oven door and went to the sink to wash his hands. The sight brought a smile.

"Be up in a minute."

DINNER WAS A SUCCESS, even if he did burn the Texas toast. Levi was pretty proud of his chicken parm and spaghetti. The semi-disaster had given them something to laugh about when, with a teasing Emily at his side, he'd scraped the top layer off the bread, slapped on some melted butter and a sprinkle of garlic powder, and called it good.

And it *was* good. For the first time in his life, he had truly enjoyed a meal at this dinner table.

Daisy ate with them and then, with a final kiss on Mason's forehead, she dashed out the door, past the skinny dog, and across the pasture.

Over the dishes, which they washed together, the lighthearted conversation continued. With baby Mason nearby, Levi pried a little deeper into Emily's life. She shared easily about her work on the town council, about how she and others hoped to build a new hospital and clinic. He told her about his ramblings and some of the funny, crazy things that happened to working cowboys.

"Is that how you damaged your knees?" She rubbed a dish towel round and round on one of Jessica's colorful blue Fiesta plates.

"Different events for each knee." He grinned down at her, even though the mentioned knees ached liked crazy after a full day and evening on his feet.

Not that he was complaining. He loved having Emily stand beside him the way Jessica probably stood next to Scott, the way a wife might.

She returned his smile, and if he wasn't mistaken, edged a bit closer to his side. "Tell me what happened."

When he scrubbed at the dishes, their arms brushed. Just a touch. Just enough to ignite his imagination.

What if she was his wife, the way she should have been? What if that baby sleeping so peacefully a few steps away was theirs?

"Levi?" She tilted her head, expression quizzical.

The fantasy evaporated like a wisp of smoke. She wasn't his. Couldn't be any more than he could tolerate living in this house where his father's voice haunted his nightly dreams. "Sorry. Wool-gathering."

"You were going to tell me how you hurt those knees. I know they bother you all the time even if you don't complain."

He didn't. Another lesson from childhood. Complaints were wasted breath.

"Well, ma'am." He drawled intentionally, keeping it light so she wouldn't think the injuries too serious. "The right knee went about a year ago. I was training a young horse when he spooked and fell with me."

"A year! Levi, if it hasn't healed by now, you've torn something that needs repair."

"Repair means healing time. I can't afford to laze around doing nothing for six or eight weeks or longer."

"You were always a hardhead about injuries. Back in high school when you stepped on that rusty sheet metal, I was so worried you'd get infection or worse, tetanus."

"Hey, I went to the doctor, and he fixed me right up."

She bumped his side. "The doctor came to you."

He remembered how important he'd felt when Emily had coerced the local doctor, a friend of her father's, to visit the high school. "Toting a needle longer than my arm."

"You needed a tetanus shot!"

"That's what Doc said." He made a silly face. "At the time, I thought your dad had paid him to do me in."

As he'd wanted her to do, Emily laughed. "When did you injure the other knee?"

"Few weeks ago. An agitated bull got me that time."

He shrugged, hands lifted, palms up. "I don't run as fast I used to."

"You really should go see the doctor."

"No can do. Afraid he'll think I'm worn out and euthanize me."

This time she snorted and bumped against him. He got the balloon in the chest thing he associated only with Emily. It felt good too.

He gazed down at her, happier than he could remember in ages. Which made no sense at all given the urgency of the position waiting in Amarillo and the fact that today he'd accepted an enormous responsibility.

He shot a look toward Mason. The little man was wide awake, staring in fascination at a set of brightly colored toys dangling from the handle of his carrier.

Something settled in Levi's chest. Something permanent and good. A commitment to Scott's boy. To *his* boy now.

He handed off the final dish and nudged his chin toward Mason. "Look who's having fun with that dangly thing you stuck on his carrier. You've been amazing with him."

"He's easy to love."

"Yeah. He is." Love. His chest swelled from it.

Quiet reigned for a few minutes, broken only by the splash of dishwater and the soft baby noises Mason made. The companionable silence caught him by surprise. He and Emily had grown comfortable together again, the way they'd been in high school. A good feeling.

Thoughts darted through his head, mostly of her, of who she'd been, of who she was now.

He pulled the plug, and water gurgled down the drain. He folded the wet dishcloth and draped it over the faucet.

When he spoke, the words were intentionally gentle, careful, so as not to offend her or send her running. "You're nuts about Mason. You've always liked kids. Even your career is about kids. Why didn't you have any?"

She turned to stash the final pan in the cabinet, and Levi suspected he'd pushed too far until she said, a soft ache in her voice, "We thought we had plenty of time."

A vise clamped his breath and squeezed hard.

Time. The ultimate thief. "I thought I had time with Scott, too."

And with you all those years ago. But he didn't say that, of course.

"Life has a way of surprising you." She took a baby bottle from the upper cabinet and set it beside a can of formula for Mason's next feeding. "But I have a great life. I'm happy and content, and what I do helps people. I've found my purpose. No complaints."

"Do you ever think about getting married again?" His words were casual conversation, but he found himself listening intently. "I mean, is there a guy in the picture?"

"Yes, to the first. No, to the last." She shrugged. "I go out now and then, but there's no spark."

"Sparks are important." Like the ones going off in his nerve endings whenever she was near. Like now.

He dried his hands and tossed the dishtowel onto the countertop. Then he reached for both of her hands. They were cool and soft against his, heated as his were by the dishwater. "Em."

Slowly, he drew her closer until he slipped his arms lightly around her waist. This time, she didn't find an excuse to move away. Her olive-green eyes lifted to his. The pupils darkened and grew larger.

He leaned in, hesitant to push but wanting to kiss her more than he could remember wanting anything in a long time. A kiss of thanks. A kiss of...he wasn't sure. All he knew was that she felt right and good in his arms.

"Em." He murmured again, chest rising and falling from the pure pleasure of her company.

"Levi." Expression sweet, she tilted her head and braced a palm along his jaw. Accepting.

Like a drowning man, he fell into her cat green eyes and ignored every roadblock and every problem that stood between him and Emily.

He kissed her.

10

Emily refused to think about all the reasons kissing Levi was not a good idea. She simply enjoyed the moment.

Light and soft, velvety too, like rose petals, his lips joined hers. She tasted vanilla ice cream, but where the dessert had been cold, the kiss was warm, tender, questioning, and maybe a little surprised.

She was surprised too. She'd not expected this. Certainly hadn't expected to want anything remotely akin to a romantic gesture from Levi Donley.

Or had she?

Over the quiet hum in her blood, Mason started to cry.

Cheeks warm, she stepped away from Levi's embrace. Reluctantly. Regretfully.

She was an adult. A grown woman. A widow who'd known the love of a fine man. But she felt as giddy as a teenager.

Levi scooped Mason from his carrier, face twisted wryly. "I guess that's what happens when you have a baby."

When you have a baby. The words pinched, a reminder of what she didn't have and what she would lose when Levi and Mason moved to Texas. Texas. A state away. A world away.

What if he stayed in Calypso too long and lost the job? What if he didn't leave?

But what if he did?

"We should get him bathed and ready for bed," she said, face still warm and blood still humming. If she didn't move away, she'd walk back into his embrace and kiss him again. "It's almost eight."

"He goes to bed that early?" He frowned. "I'm still outside working at that time, especially in the long days of summer."

"Raising a baby requires adjustments. I wrote out his schedule for you."

He didn't say anything else as he carried the baby upstairs. Was he having second thoughts? Or simply mulling the other unknown obstacles in his future?

Emily followed a few stair steps behind. With Daisy's help, they'd brought all of Mason's belongings up to the nursery before dinner and sorted through the chest of drawers Jessica had packed full of tiny garments. The heartrending, sobering task reminded them of the couple who had lovingly placed each item in this room but would never see them used.

Many of the clothes were too small already, and Emily had bagged them to donate to foster families.

Jessica, a former foster child herself, would have approved.

Now, as they bathed the baby and readied him for his first night at home in weeks, Levi cleared his throat.

"Em." With both hands holding Mason while she washed the wiggling infant, he captured her gaze over the white baby tub. "About that kiss."

If he apologized, she'd dump this tub of water on his thick head.

Before he could say more, she waved him off. "A kiss, Levi. No big deal."

A furrow appeared in his forehead. He blinked but held her gaze another minute before refocusing on the slippery boy. For a while, he said nothing else, and the atmosphere grew tense.

What was that about?

She didn't know and couldn't let herself think beyond the here and now. With practiced ease, she fell into social worker mode and began to recite instructions about Mason's routine.

"If you have any problems, or even if you aren't sure about something, text me, call me. Day or night." She put a wet hand on Levi's forearm to get his attention. "Promise you will, or I'll worry."

"Wouldn't want that."

His skin was warm and smooth, the muscles hard and strong. Arms that had held her close downstairs. Arms strong enough to tame a horse or toss a calf but tender enough to bathe an infant.

Arms she wanted around her again.

She had to stop thinking like this!

Mason churned his chubby legs. Water splashed her face. She jerked to one side. Grateful for the break from her bizarre thoughts, she laughed. Levi snorted, so Emily splashed him in teasing revenge.

With a low growl, eyes narrowed in amused threat, he returned the favor. By the time Mason's bath ended, they were both damp and laughing, water droplets shining on their faces. Feeling good. Working together like a couple. And if in those few moments Emily felt like a mother and a wife, she wasn't sorry.

"We'll both need a change of shirts after this." Levi grimaced at his very wet western shirt and then at her soaked blouse. Fortunately, the dark color wasn't see-through, but she shivered a little from the chill.

Levi hitched an eyebrow. "Cold?"

"A little water never hurt anyone."

"Not mad at me then?"

Not about the water fight. "It was fun."

"Yeah, it was, wasn't it?"

"Don't look so pleased with yourself. There is still a lot of water in this tub."

He laughed. A real, hearty, happy sound that filled her senses and brought laughter bubbling up in her own throat.

"Oh, Em. Em."

He extended a towel, the big grin fading to a soft, appealing smile. He seemed so much more relaxed tonight than he had in previous weeks. Did she dare hope he was settling in? That he might put the past behind him and find contentment here?

Or was she being a foolish woman who could easily get her heart stomped again?

While she blotted the excess moisture from her shirt, Emily watched with an odd catch beneath her ribcage while strong but tender cowboy hands dried the sweet little baby and dressed him in one-piece footed pajamas. A cartoon horse decorated the blue front.

"Not bad for a novice, huh?" he asked proudly as he swaddled Mason in soft flannel and formed a snuggly bundle. "He looks like a burrito."

As if insulted, Mason opened his mouth and howled.

Startled, the adults exchanged looks and snickered.

"He's not happy with that remark, cowboy."

"You think he's hungry?"

"Not for burritos." She stroked the side of her finger along the baby's cheek. He eagerly turned in the direction of her touch. "Time for a bottle, a rocking chair, and a cozy bed."

Mason's cry grew louder.

Levi jerked a thumb toward the door. "I'll run downstairs for his bottle."

"Coward. You just want to escape the crying."

He was already moving toward the hallway. "Busted!"

Feeling mellow, Emily snuggled the crying baby close and settled in the rocker, heart full. As she'd done every night for weeks, she began to rock and sing. Mason quieted in seconds, dark eyes glued to her face.

Tonight had been good. Too good.

She didn't hear the footsteps on the stairs, but she felt a presence and glanced up. The tall cowboy leaned against the door frame, watching her. His expression stopped her breath. Was the tenderness for her? For Mason? Or for both of them?

"That was beautiful. And effective." He pushed off and turned over the baby bottle. "I'd forgotten how well you sing."

Her pulse fluttered. Silly, foolish pulse. "I love singing to him."

She shouldn't have said that. She had no right to pretend she was anything but the social worker.

But she couldn't deny what was in her heart.

"That settles it then." Levi crouched beside the rocker. A knee popped. He winced and braced the painful joint with one hand. "Since I have a voice like a frog, you have to come out every night and sing him to sleep."

She'd love to do exactly that, but what about when he was no longer here? Who would sing to Mason then? And how would her grieving heart ever heal again?

Rather than dwell on questions she couldn't answer, Emily dipped her chin toward the infant. "You and this bottle of formula have made him very happy."

Mason's eyelids dropped shut while he suckled the bottle. By the time the formula disappeared, his mouth lolled open, and he was ready to settle for the night.

Levi lifted the infant from her arms and carefully positioned him in the crib on his back.

Emily reached for the night light, clicked it on, and shut off the rocking horse lamp. The room faded to semi-darkness.

Her lips curved. "You remembered the correct positioning."

"I have a great teacher." Their voices were quiet

murmurs. "Baby on his back close toward the end of the crib for safety. No pillow or toys or piles of blankets that might smother him."

She shuddered. "What an awful thought."

"Yeah." The word was barely a whisper, and she knew that he, like she, was thinking of Scott and Jessica.

"I miss her tremendously, Levi. I cannot imagine how much you must ache for your brother."

He turned his head so that he was cast in shadowy relief. "Does it ever get easier? Losing someone you love?"

Emily swallowed. She understood the question. He asked about Dennis, about her husband's untimely death. "The awful, throat clutching, scream-in-the night grief eventually diminishes, but the ache of sorrow is always there." She pressed two fingers to her chest. "You don't forget or replace people you love."

"Is it worth it, then?" His voice was quiet, pensive. "To love so deeply?"

She put a hand on his arm. "Yes. Oh yes. Love is worth the pain."

She heard the echo of her words inside her head. Love *was* worth the loss. To give love, to be loved, to share God's greatest, most powerful emotion with another human being. Even if that person eventually went away.

She knew then, there in that shadowy room with a baby sleeping nearby, that she was in love with Levi Donley. Maybe some part of her always had been.

He must have felt her mood shift. He shifted too, a quiet rustle in the dim room. His arm came around her shoulders, and he snugged her close to his sturdy, muscled side, holding her there, safe and secure. Until that last day fourteen years ago, she'd always been safe with Levi.

She turned into his chest and let him hold her. She shouldn't. She was opening herself to heartbreak. But for the first time since Dennis's death, she felt like more than a social worker and a dutiful sister. She felt like a woman who could love again.

Love. A dangerous, dangerous word. Hadn't she vowed never to be that vulnerable again? Especially since Levi didn't love her. Not enough to face his dragons on this ranch and make a life here. He had other plans for Mason and himself. Plans that didn't include her.

Was being with him and Mason temporarily enough? Could she risk loving and losing them both?

Love is always worth the risk. Wasn't that what she'd said? Was God tapping at her closed and fearful heart to open it up again?

Levi's heart beat against hers, and she lifted her eyes, wanting more than she dared ask. There would always be the issue of his father between them. An issue he wouldn't even discuss. And there was still the issue of Texas.

Was she being a fool?

Love is always worth the risk.

"About those sparks," Levi said gently, dented chin tilted down to look into her eyes.

Her heartbeat answered his, thrumming faster and faster.

His lips curved as he leaned close until their breath mingled and his firm, manly mouth captured hers.

This kiss was different from the earlier one. It was more than a question. It was a wish fulfilled.

THE NEXT MORNING, Slim Donley's yell didn't jerk Levi from his slumber. Mason's did.

With a surprising amount of sunlight streaming between the curtains, Levi shook out the cobwebs and stumbled across the hall into the nursery.

Yesterday's perfectly adorable baby flailed his arms and legs in absolute fury. Exactly as he'd done twice in the night.

No wonder Levi hadn't had the dream. He hadn't been asleep long enough.

Screaming baby in tow, he bounded down the stairs and into the kitchen. With Mason under one arm like a really noisy football, Levi prepared the bottle. He'd barely popped the nipple into the toothless mouth and collapsed in the downstairs rocker when a knock sounded on the door.

The skinny dog gave a soft woof.

"Better check it out, Mason," he grumbled. "We don't need any dog bites." Not that he expected the stray to bite. He was probably too weak. And yet, he'd been a bit of a tiger at Beech's place.

Levi opened the door to find Daisy, dressed in jeans and a green T-shirt with a backpack over her shoulders, feeding bacon to the skinny stray.

She looked up at Levi with a bright smile. How did the kid always manage to look cheerful with Beech for a father?

Daisy didn't wait to be invited. She stepped right in. "I like your dog."

"He's not mine."

"He wants to be. You should keep him. I think his name should be Buttercup."

Levi's eyebrows shot up. "Buttercup?"

"Uh-huh. Buttercup. See? He agrees." She rubbed the animal's bony head. Adoring canine eyes the color of gold looked from child to man and back again. The whip-thin tail never stopped moving.

Levi was too exhausted this morning to think about dog names.

"Can I hold him?"

"The dog?"

Daisy giggled, as he'd intended. "Mason, silly. I thought you might need some help, this being your first day on the job and all."

What was she, nine going on thirty? "Smart kid. But don't you have school?"

"I'm ready. I got up extra early this morning to do chores so I could come over and help out."

She plopped down on the couch and extended both arms. "I'll bet he's wet."

"I'll bet you're right. I haven't changed him yet. You feed him, and I'll go upstairs for the diapers."

"Might as well bring a bunch down here and save the trips. Your knees can't take it."

He looked at the third grader in wonder. How could she be that mature? "How old did you say you were again? Thirty-five?"

She giggled and hunched her shoulders. "Nine, silly

cowboy."

Levi returned with a full bag of disposable diapers. "I should probably put his playpen down here too."

"Uh-huh. And his swing. You need one of those sling things too. I saw them on TV. You can carry Mason anywhere you go."

That was actually a great idea. He could work and hang with his nephew at the same time.

"I think there's one upstairs." At least that's what he thought the apparatus was. There were at least a dozen baby items he had no idea what to do with. "You want some coffee?"

She looked at him as if he'd grown another head and then giggled again. "I'm too little to drink coffee."

"Oh, yeah. I keep forgetting you're not forty yet."

To her continued giggle, he staggered into the kitchen and set the coffee brewing, then returned with a glass of orange juice. "Here you go."

Out on the porch, the skinny dog woofed again. A car door slammed.

This time when he opened the door, he set out a bowl of dog food.

Emily stepped up on the porch. "You're getting attached to him."

"I always wanted a dog." He rubbed a hand over his uncombed hair. "What are you doing out here so early?"

"Checking." Her gaze slid over his whiskery face, rumpled T-shirt, and sweats, then slid all the way down to his bare feet. "Looks like you had a rough night."

"We'll get the hang of things."

Emily stopped in the doorway and peered at the

couch where Daisy sat feeding Mason. "You have good help."

"I do. Want some coffee? Or juice?"

"I'll get it."

"Get me some too." He collapsed on the sofa next to the children.

Emily snorted but returned with two mugs. "Black with two sugars, right?"

He took the cup gratefully. "I didn't really expect—"

Emily patted him on the head like a child. "I know. Otherwise you wouldn't have gotten it."

He sipped the scalding brew and sighed. "This is nice. Two ladies to take care of Mason while I wake up with a hot cup."

"Don't get used to it." Emily, bracketing her mug with both hands, settled across from him on an armchair.

He didn't bother to ask for reasons. He knew. Once he departed Calypso, he and Mason were on their own. Scary. But not as scary as staying.

"I'll come over every day if you want me to, Levi." Daisy's pert face was eager and intense. "I can babysit while you work the ranch."

"Don't you need to be in school?"

The child made a face.

Emily answered for her. "Yes, she does. Every day. Including today. What time does your bus run, Daisy?"

With a comical, put-upon sigh, Daisy returned the baby to Levi's arms and got to her feet. "I gotta go."

Emily's coffee cup clicked against the table. "Want to ride with me this morning?"

Daisy perked up. "Could I?"

"Grab your bag, and I'll drop you at the school. I have an early appointment with the principal anyway."

Levi frowned and followed her into the kitchen. "You just got here."

"I came by to be sure everything was going okay. You appear to have things under control." She rinsed out her cup and set it in the sink.

Levi had a quick rewind to last night's kitchen kisses. He wouldn't mind repeating them right here and now. If Daisy wasn't staring at them from the entryway.

"Nothing's under control. I mean, it is. Sort of. Mason is fine. Daisy's fine. The dog is fine. Me, I could use some bacon and eggs. If you'll come back, I'll cook for us."

Expression amused, she patted his chest. "I can't, but thanks for asking."

"Lunch maybe?" he asked, desperate to keep her here.

She seemed to consider the idea. "I'll text you. You text me if you have any issues."

The issue was somewhere between his neck and his belly button. A little thing called his heart.

"Em." The baby between them, he turned to face her, effectively blocking Daisy's view. In a lowered voice, he said, "I enjoyed last night. With you."

His gaze dropped to her mouth.

Emily's cheeks tinged pink. "Me, too."

"Maybe we could...do something together."

"We're together practically every day."

"You know what I mean. Something special." A memory to take with him. Something good to replace the last time they'd parted. "I want to say thanks for all you've done."

She put her hand on Mason's back and nodded, the action curt. "I'll think about it."

While he wondered if he'd said something wrong, she hustled Daisy to the SUV. He followed, opening and closing doors and wishing she would stay.

With the baby making soft noises against his neck, Levi watched the woman and the little girl drive way. He raised his free hand and was rewarded with Daisy's vigorous wave and a quick honk of Emily's horn.

Squinting until they disappeared, he heaved a happy sigh. The skinny dog bumped his leg, and he dropped the free hand to the bony head. What would he do with the dog when he moved to Texas? The shepherd-lab mix was quiet around the cows and horses, and friendly, though he never failed to give a warning *yip* when a car arrived. He was a good dog. He didn't deserve to be abandoned again.

"What do you think, Butter?" Levi asked. "Ever been to Texas?"

11

A week passed in a blur. Between diapers and bottles and cows and ranch repair, Levi fell into bed every night exhausted, aware that he'd be up again for a two o'clock feeding, and if the Lord had mercy, Mason would sleep again until six. Babies, he'd learned quickly, were not as easy as calves and colts.

This particularly sunny day, he had errands in town, including a visit to the Calypso Assisted Living Center and Great Aunt Ruby. Time for Mason to meet the most influential woman in Uncle Levi's life.

First stop was Hammond's Feed Store for dog food, where he spent fifteen minutes talking shop with Ace and Nate before heading out to their sister's house. The social worker's home reminded him of her—modern and elegant with a two-car garage, a small, tidy lawn, and a brick archway leading up to the door. Very different from the Triple C's ranch-style dormer where she'd grown up.

Before Levi had a chance to take Mason from the car

seat, Emily exited the house and strode toward him, black hair shining in the sun. In tan slacks and a white blouse with a kelly green cardigan, she looked spring-time fresh, vibrant and eye-catching.

Every nerve ending in his body vibrated. Sparks erupted as if a Fourth of July celebration were going on inside his brain.

Since Mason's first night home, he and Emily had spent every evening together, and if he kissed her hello, goodbye, and a few times in between, so what? They both knew the score. Too much dirty water flowed under their collective bridges to ever get across the chasm.

But nothing said they couldn't enjoy their time together.

He leaned across the truck seat and pushed the door open.

"Hi." She slid into the cab and immediately turned toward the infant in the backseat. "Hi, sugar bear."

Mason made appropriate noises and wind-milled his arms and legs.

"Thanks for going with me." Levi's remark turned her attention to him.

"I haven't been to see Ruby in a while, not since she was in the hospital last time."

The hospital. Another reason for him to feel guilty. He hadn't even known his great aunt had missed Scott's funeral because of illness.

He put the truck in gear and backed down the driveway into the street. "The nurse said she's fit and feisty today."

Emily plopped a tiny brown purse on the truck

console and angled toward him, eyes intensely green above the cardigan. "You brought flowers. Good call."

Flowers seemed the least he could do. A colorful spring bouquet of daisies and tulips to make his great-aunt smile. "Think she'll like them?"

"She's female. Of course, she'll like them."

He wanted to slap his forehead. Why hadn't he considered buying flowers for Emily, too? Two nights ago, he'd taken her out to Turf and Surf for dinner, where Mason had attracted the attention of every waitress and half the patrons. Though his hope for a quiet, romantic dinner was shot all to pieces, they'd had fun anyway. Anyplace with Emily was a good time.

He should have sent flowers the next day.

"What are you frowning about?" Emily tapped an index finger between her eyes.

Levi scrubbed at the frown. "Nothing. Will you have time for lunch after?"

"I should. My appointments don't begin until one."

"You're still coming to the house tonight, right?"

Her smile was enigmatic. "What's in it for me?"

He pumped his eyebrows. "What do you have in mind?"

Emily pulled a silly face. "Diapers, rocking chair, maybe some food if you're in the mood to try online recipes again."

"You must have read my mind." Levi glanced her way with a wicked grin. "At least part of it."

She whacked his arm, and they both laughed.

Weird and totally uncharacteristic to feel so undeniably chipper for absolutely no reason at all.

The ride from Emily's home to The Assisted Living Center took less than fifteen minutes, including a traffic stop at what he'd dubbed *the light of many minutes*—the only stoplight in Calypso.

When they arrived, Emily insisted on carrying Mason inside while Levi brought up the rear with a load of baby gear. On her wise advice, he'd learned never to go anywhere without all the necessities. Babies were unpredictable.

Bypassing the nursing station, they entered Ruby's living quarters. Though small, the studio apartment was homey and comfortable.

The tiny, frail woman sat in a lift chair with a red plaid throw across her legs and a warm smile on her thin, weathered face. Her white hair was brushed back in a tidy bun just the way he remembered. Except in those days, her hair had been brown.

"Well, praise my Jesus. Look who's here."

Levi leaned in for a cheek kiss. She smelled like baby powder. "Brought a couple of stragglers to see you, Auntie."

She and Emily exchanged pleasantries before Ruby reached for the baby. "Oh, would you look at this, Levi? He has your chin."

"And Scott's fat cheeks," he said.

"He'll outgrow those like his daddy did." Ruby smoothed a fingertip over each of the baby's eyebrows. "He has his daddy's big eyes too. I notice them now that he's a little older. Jessica brought him to see me, you know, that first week." Her eyes filled with tears. "She was such a sweet girl."

"I wish I'd known her." He said the words he'd thought a dozen times, and all the while, his conscience pounded him. He should have remained close. He should have been here. He should have known. "She did a great job with the house."

Ruby's sharp gaze settled on him. "You doing all right out there?"

If he didn't count the relentless memories, the dream of his father's angry voice, the images of that last, horrible day when he'd raised a fist to his own flesh-and-blood father.

Avoiding the question, he tugged a chair close to his aunt and sat, keeping the worse knee straight. In his rush to see Emily and Aunt Ruby, he'd forgotten the ibuprofen this morning.

Emily claimed the armchair on Ruby's left side.

"Emily's a good teacher."

"Sure is good to see the two of you together again. The way it should be."

Levi let that slide too, but he noticed the slight flush on Emily's porcelain skin.

"She's helping Mason and I adjust, and there's this little neighbor girl and a stray dog who keep me entertained." He launched into a detailed description of Daisy and Butter.

"They've both laid claim to Mason. Daisy's there morning and evening. And Butter, I'm telling you, Auntie, that dog is part human. Anytime I'm working outside, I take Mason along. When I put him in his stroller thing, Butter lies right beside him and doesn't move unless

Mason cries. Then he dances circles around my legs and whines until I do something."

"Dog like that's a keeper."

"Yes, ma'am. I think so too. Always wanted a dog."

"I remember." Ruby's look was sympathetic. She knew. She'd been his rescuer as much as Slim would allow. No one, not even a determined woman like Ruby, interfered with the Donley Ranch work force. Another reminder of why he couldn't stay in his town. Going to church hadn't resolved his hatred for his father, and being here in Calypso made it worse.

He rolled his Stetson around in his hands. "Got a job offer out in the Texas Panhandle. Ranch manager with all the benefits."

Ruby's thin hands stilled. "Oh?"

That was Ruby. Open the door and let him spill his guts. The only thing in his youth he'd kept from her was the one thing he'd never told a soul. Humiliation didn't sit well on his shoulders.

He told her about the job, aware that Emily was quiet, her eyes on his face. He avoided looking at her.

"Are you going to take it then?"

"If I can sell the ranch and get to Texas before Parnell hires someone else."

"That's what you want for you and Mason? Living on someone else's ranch, building their future instead of your own? Instead of his?"

"Never thought of it that way." He planned to save the sale proceeds for Mason. Wouldn't that count as building a future? "It's a great job, Auntie, doing what I'm good at."

Ranch work was all he knew, and if he got tired of a

certain place, he could pull up and move on. Like always. Except, now there was Mason to consider, and moving around didn't sound as promising as it once had.

"Something to pray about." Ruby jiggled Mason's reaching hand. "Just be sure you don't let old ghosts scare you away from what you really want."

He would have scoffed, except he knew exactly what she was talking about.

HOURS LATER, still mulling his aunt's advice, Levi drove Emily back to her house on the Triple C. Mason had conked out in the back seat, his head bent to one side. If an adult slept like that, he'd wake with the king of all cricks. Babies were made of rubber. Rubber and strange, ejecting liquids. Or so it seemed to Levi.

"Want to come in for some iced tea?" Emily asked when he opened the pickup door for her. He helped her down and stood with his hands bracketing her narrow waist, reluctant to let her go.

He didn't want any iced tea. He wanted to kiss her, hold her, and keep her with him a while longer. But considering the conversation with his aunt, the action was probably selfish. Real selfish. If he was leaving town soon, and he was, why did he want to be with Emily so badly?

Levi kissed the top of her head and dropped his hold. He did not, however, step away. "Too full. Burger Barn still makes the biggest burger in the county."

The whole truth was more complicated. He needed some alone time to think. Ruby had rattled his cage. She was wise. He trusted her. But she didn't know the whole story.

Emily placed her palm on the front of his shirt. He felt the uptick in his pulse. "Today was nice. I enjoyed seeing Ruby, and she seemed thrilled to have you there with Mason. We should bring her out to your ranch some night for dinner. I can cook if you'd like."

His heart turned over. Emily. Thoughtful, generous Emily. "Or, if the weather's nice, we can cook out. Scott has a grill in the shed."

Finding Scott's shiny, stainless grill had surprised him. Slim Donley would never have considered buying a device meant for family enjoyment.

Pleasure bloomed in Emily's eyes. "That sounds fun. Shrimp kabobs, potato salad, homemade ice cream. Maybe Connie will bake a blackberry cobbler, and we can make it a little party."

"I doubt there's ever been a party at the Donley Ranch."

The incessant Oklahoma wind ruffled her hair and rustled the leaves of a nearby maple tree. "Why else would there be a grill?"

The statement gave him pause. Parties and fun at the Donley Ranch? Laughter? Good times?

The notion seeped into his consciousness like a healing balm. Their boyhoods had been the same, but somehow Scott had managed to put the pain behind him and grab hold of the good life.

Was that because of Jessica? Or because of God?

Love and faith must be powerful antidotes.

They talked another minute, the sun shining so pretty

on Emily's hair that Levi looped it behind her ears just for an excuse to touch the black silk.

"Why not come to the ranch now?" he asked. He could think later. Or not at all.

"I have a home visit in Rock Springs and a little paperwork to finish first."

"I thought this was supposed to be a day off."

"It is, but I'm doing this couple a favor." She tiptoed up and kissed his chin. "See you later, Unc."

She spun and trotted on white Keds up the short side-walk to the front door. Levi waited, enjoying the sight of her until she waved and disappeared inside the house.

With a sigh of contentment, he rounded the truck. Opening the door, he peered in the back to be sure Mason still slept. Satisfied, he stepped up. His cell phone vibrated. He backed away, not wanting to disturb the infant, and fished the device from his hip pocket.

One glance at the caller ID and his full belly dipped halfway to his knees. Jack Parnell. They'd talked last week. The rancher was growing impatient.

Levi answered. They traded polite greetings before Jack got down to business.

"I guess you know why I'm calling."

"I do. And I appreciate your patience while I get things ironed out here in Calypso."

"Well, see, that's what I'm calling about. I got an application for the position from another cowboy I respect."

The muscles across Levi's back bunched into knots. "Are you withdrawing the offer?"

"Not yet. But I need to know something solid, Levi. I realize you've had a tough go lately, and I'm sorry as a man can be, but cows don't wait, and this is business. The other cowboy has some loose ends, too, so we'll talk again at the end of the month. If you want to be my manager, I need you on The Long Spur before then. What do you say?"

The end of the month didn't seem long enough. He had plans. Emily had plans. And the ranch still hadn't sold. He didn't even have a sign out front.

He licked dry lips and gazed up into the blue heavens, wishing someone would write the answers across the sky.

"Levi? You still there?"

"Yes, sir. Still here." And he shouldn't be. He should be in Texas. He hated this place. Didn't he? Aunt Ruby and her ghost had put doubts in his mind.

He cleared his throat. "I'll be there."

12

Emily was mad enough to chew bricks. And more than a little shaken.

She'd been having a great day until now. Sunshine, no wind, in a state known for its hearty breezes, the drift of honeysuckle on the air, bluebirds perched on a wire fence. Her favorite time of year. But nature's beauty was lost to her at the moment. Thanks to Daisy's father.

Of all the jerks she'd ever met, and she'd met plenty in her line of work, Arlo Beech owned the grand prize.

Sucking back long gulps of fury and a good dose of anxiety, she drove away from his farm.

The cretin. The unmitigated, mean-spirited, hateful excuse for a human being.

At the intersection, fingers still shaky against the steering wheel, she changed directions and pulled down the long driveway to the Donley Ranch. She was close by, might as well stop in and say hello. Yes, it was an excuse. Right now, she needed a friend. She needed Levi.

Emily slammed out of the vehicle, annoyed that her legs wobbled. She started toward the front porch but stopped when she saw movement near the horse barn. The yellow dog spotted her and woofed.

Levi glanced up and waved. He was in the corral, a hose aimed at a water trough. Mason snuggled close to the cowboy's chest in a baby sling.

Some of Emily's anxiety leaked out. Tenderness moved in. For the baby. For the man.

The yellow dog moseyed out to meet her. She dropped a hand to his head. "Hi, Butter."

Mouth open in pleasure, the sweet stray followed her back to the corral.

Levi twisted the faucet closed and wrapped the hose around a wheel mounted on the side of the barn. "Be with you in a sec."

"No rush." She opened the corral and went inside, relieved to be in Levi's company. Secure. Protected.

"What's up?" Levi ambled toward her across the loose dirt, a slight limp betraying the knee that wouldn't heal. The bad knee was doing well, mending. The worse knee, as he called it, not so much. She needed to nag him to see a doctor until he took action.

"I was in the neighborhood." A joke, of course, given the rural nature of his ranch and that of Arlo Beech.

As Levi drew near, his steps faltered. He stopped, tilted his head and studied her. His eyes narrowed. "Are you okay?"

Emily pushed a lock of hair behind one ear. "I am now."

"What happened? You're pale." Cowboy-strong hands gripped her upper arms. "And you're shaking."

She shouldn't tell him. He'd be angry. But she knew she would. She needed to.

"I paid an official visit to Daisy's dad. She's missed school twice this week. Her absences are becoming a serious problem."

A scowl pulled his eyebrows together. "She was here this morning. I assumed she was headed to school."

"She wasn't. He kept her home to help with the plowing."

Levi's jaw clenched and unclenched. "I've been over there. The guy is a first-class goon. What did he say that upset you?"

"Nothing I haven't heard before."

"Tell me."

So she did, spilling out the vitriolic conversation minus the worst swear words. She didn't even want to think those.

Levi stepped closer, into her personal space, shielding her. "He was toting a rifle, wasn't he? That's what scared you."

Mason stirred. Emily placed a hand on the baby's back. "How did you know?"

"Seems to be his motis operandi. He didn't point it at you, did he?"

She swallowed. The gun had scared her, and Beech had seen the fear and held the rifle waist high, a mean little grin on his lips. The veiled threat had been enough to shake her. But Emily didn't share that information with Levi. Heat and anger already emanated from him. She didn't want him doing something crazy.

"No. He didn't point it at me. Nothing like that. He was all talk. Saying if I knew what was good for me, I'd mind my own business." Emily rubbed Mason's cheek with one finger, drawing comfort from the content child. "Don't worry about it. It's no big deal."

Levi's scowl deepened. "What did he mean by that?"

"Nothing, probably. An empty threat by a small man. Now that I'm here, reviewing the incident with you, I think I over-reacted."

"Or not." His fists clenched and unclenched. She shouldn't have told him. "Maybe we should report this to the sheriff."

"No." Not a good idea at all. Lawson Hawk was a friend of her brothers. If she told the sheriff, Ace and Nate would hear about the incident and go nuts. "A man has a right to carry a rifle on his own property. He didn't threaten to shoot me or do anything physical. I don't think he's that crazy. He was just so hateful and rude. I worry for Daisy."

"Me too."

Emily blew out the last of her nerves in a gusty breath. She was better now. With Levi.

"But Daisy seems happy, and never once has anyone seen a bruise on her. I've asked."

"I still don't like the way he treated you." He tugged her up as close as he could with a baby hanging between them. Mason squirmed and grunted. "Come in the house.

Let me fix you a Coke. Feed you cookies. Rub your feet. Anything to make you feel better."

She felt better already.

"Levi, really." She stroked the sleeve of his denim shirt, soothing both of them at the same time. "I'm okay."

She was tougher than that, and she'd had irate people swear at her before. But when Levi persisted, endearingly kind, she followed him toward the house. A little pampering by a handsome cowboy sounded good right now.

LEVI CONSIDERED HIS OPTIONS. He could call the sheriff, call Nate and Ace, ride over and beat the meanness out of Arlo Beech, or take care of Emily in the here and now.

The latter seemed most pleasant and least likely to end in a jail sentence, so he ushered her into the house. He couldn't help wondering what Emily might be keeping from him in the interest of peace. For certain, the dirt bag of a neighbor had scared her.

He filled a glass with cola, waited until the foam settled, added some more, and then carried it to her. She'd plopped down on the couch as if her knees wouldn't hold her any longer. The notion made him madder.

Gratefully, Emily took the glass and sipped. Her fingers trembled the slightest bit. That made him madder still.

Levi tugged a chair up in front of her and sat so their knees touched. Lately, he'd used any excuse to touch her, but right now, she seemed to need the connection more than he did.

She'd been afraid, and she'd come to him. That had to mean something. Probably that he was the closest friendly face.

While she drank and got her bearings, he got up again and unharnessed the baby, kissed his forehead and placed him in the playpen. Daisy had been right. Having the portable crib in the living room saved him a million trips upstairs. In fact, the whole living room looked like a nursery. Life was easier this way.

Moving around behind the sofa, he massaged Emily's shoulders. She rolled her head back to look at him. "You can do that all day. And my feet tomorrow."

Levi grinned down into the green eyes. "I charge by the minute."

"Sold." Her eyes dropped shut. She made a little moaning sound that sent his mind into places he tried to stay out of. If she was his wife, he could think anything he wanted.

His kneading hands paused. Where had that come from? Emily wasn't his wife, never could be. She was way above his pay grade.

He dropped his hands to his side and stepped back. Emily opened her eyes. His chest tightened. She sure did crazy things to his head.

"Want to go for a ride?" Yeah. A ride in the fields and woods, along the ponds and creek with the wind blowing in his face. That would erase his wild thoughts and Emily's stress. He wanted her to feel better and to forget Arlo Beech and his nasty mouth.

"Sounds good. I have a ton of paperwork waiting, but I could use some fresh air to clear my head."

That made two of them.

WHEN HE'D SADDLED the horses—Freckles and a quiet Palomino he called Goldie—Levi led them to the front porch and texted Emily that he was outside, waiting. She was upset enough for one day. No way he expected her to come inside the hated barn.

She exited the house in too-long jeans, a bright blue shirt, and western boots she must have gotten from Jessica's closet. One of these days, he'd clean that out. So far, he'd not had the heart to go through Scott's belongings either.

"Looking good, Miss Caldwell."

"Jessica wouldn't mind." She handed off Mason and swung into the saddle with the natural ease of a woman who'd ridden all her life. Then she reached back for the baby.

"You sure? I can carry him."

"Are you kidding?" She patted the sling around her shoulders. "I'm already dressed for the occasion. Gimme that precious angel."

He lifted the child into her arms and held the palomino while she made the adjustments. Mason cooed happy noises and grinned at her.

"Look at him." Levi offered up the reins. "Already charming the ladies."

"Like uncle, like nephew." Emily tapped the palomino's sides and moseyed away, leaving Levi to stare after her straight back.

She thought he was charming? Him? After the heartache and humiliation he'd brought to her door? After years of silence?

He gave Freckles a heel tap and trotted after the woman and child. "Was that a compliment?"

She glanced over her shoulder with a mild expression. "I believe you're one of the most clueless humans I've ever met."

What was that supposed to mean?

And what happened to charming?

Freckles, never to be out-distanced, pulled alongside Goldie, and they moseyed side by side across the spring grass. Butter trotted ahead, nose to the ground and thin tail swinging like a gate in a gale.

Levi sure liked that dog. Like Ruby said, a keeper.

He sat back in the saddle, content and relaxed. The rains had turned everything a rich, fertile kelly green, and the ponds were full and shiny in the sunlight. Black cattle swished their tails and grazed, growing fatter by the day. The biggest repairs were completed, and the small ones would get there before the end of the month.

The Donley Ranch was market-ready, lock, stock, and barrel. He should be happy about that, but something niggled at him; something didn't feel right.

Emily broke into his thoughts. "I've always loved this pasture and that little line of woods along the creek."

He gazed at the side of her face, the way she sat a horse like a pro and held the reins lightly. That she loved anything about the Donley Ranch shocked him.

"Remember when we snuck down there one night

after your chores were done and fished in the moon-light?" she asked, voice nostalgic.

Snuck was right. Moonlight. Starlight. Emily. "Fished? Was that what we were doing?"

A flush tinged her cheekbones. "Yes, it was, silly."

He laughed. "I remember. It must have been eleven o'clock or later, but I caught three baby perch, and you caught a nice bass, maybe three pounds."

"And got so many chiggers, I itched for a month."

"Good times." The words were out before he'd realized what he said. Words from the heart. There *had* been good times, and being with Emily reminded him that not every memory of this ranch was bitter. "We should do it again. You, me, my little partner there, and fishing poles."

"And lots of bug spray."

They shared a grin and rode on a while without talking, comfortable together in a way he'd never expected. He and Emily. *The way it should be.* Ruby's statement rattled around in the loose shell intended for his brain.

Without pre-planning, he guided Freckles toward the creek and woods. Emily noticed and shot him a smile. A really big smile, as if she were happy, as if she enjoyed his company here on this place that had changed the direction of both their lives.

His chest ballooned.

She pointed toward a patch of Indian Paintbrush, the bright coral blooms like a carpet over the grass. He didn't tell her that they'd have to be mowed. She knew they were weeds that choked out pasture grass, but she'd always liked them.

He pulled Freckles to a halt and slid to the ground,

where he picked a handful. Butter, exploring up ahead, circled back to him and waited, mouth agape and golden eyes bright with adoration. How did anyone discard such a loving dog? Levi smoothed a hand over the floppy ears before handing up the flowers.

"For the beautiful lady. Don't sniff them. You'll sneeze."

Expression pleased, Emily stuck the stems through the hole in the saddle's pommel. "Thank you."

They weren't roses or a spring bouquet from the florist, but she liked them. Yeah. And he liked her.

He couldn't decide if that was a good thing or a bad thing.

Probably a stupid thing.

Levi touched the baby's foot, more as an excuse to stay close to Emily than anything. "Mason seems to be enjoying the ride."

She dipped her head to look into the sleeping face. "He's an easy baby."

The look of love on her face was soft and tender, the look of a mother for her child. Mason would never know that kind of love.

One more worry. Being a dad to an orphaned baby had more potholes than an unmarked county road.

The saddle creaked as he mounted and reseated. "You think he'll miss having a mother?"

He thought about the question a lot.

"Did you?"

"Yeah. I always wished she was there, that I had a mom like other kids." He pointed to a yellow butterfly flitting in front of them before continuing. "I kind of remember my mother, but not very well. She had long brown hair. Other than that, she's all fuzzy."

He sure didn't remember anyone ever looking at him the way Emily looked at Mason. No one had ever sung to him either, or heard his bedtime prayers, or kissed his boo-boos.

"I would love to have known my mother, too, but it's hard to miss someone you never knew." Emily kissed the top of Mason's head, and the balloon in Levi's chest almost exploded. "Connie's been a mother to all of us Caldwell kids. In fact, it's always seemed as if she *is* my mother. We were blessed to have her."

"Did she sing to you the way you do for Mason?" Weird that he would ask that, but her singing to his nephew soothed a bruised place in his heart. He didn't want the little cowboy to have bruises or hurts or a life of regrets.

"Oh, yes. I know all kinds of Spanish lullabies and kids' songs."

"Was that what you were singing to Mason the other night?"

"Probably."

Mason needed a mother to sing to him. In these few weeks, the little cowboy had had Emily. Would something in his tiny psyche remember? Or would he, like Levi, grow up with an empty hole where his mama should be?

"My singing's lousy, but I can teach him to pray," he said. And doctor his skinned knees and hug him when he cried. "I don't know anything about mothering." He wished he did.

One hand on the reins and the other on Mason's back, Emily turned her head. "You care, Levi. That's the most important thing."

Yeah, he cared. Love for that tiny human being had slammed him in the gut like a wrecking ball. He'd do anything, *anything,* to give Mason the happy childhood he hadn't experienced himself.

Anything? You'd even live here and raise him on the Donley Ranch where his Daddy and Mama were happy? You'd bury your ghosts and let go of the anger?

The questions came unbidden, as if someone else had said them inside his head. He didn't want to answer.

They entered the copse of trees, mostly blackjack and cottonwood and a few blooming redbud and dogwood. The woods smelled fertile and moist and scented with spring blossoms of unknown origin. Shade and whispering creek water cooled the temperature.

"Is he warm enough?"

Emily touched Mason's cheeks. "He's fine. It's not that cool, and he's snug against me."

"Lucky kid."

Emily ignored him. "Is that the same rock where we went fishing?"

"Looks like it."

She reined Goldie to a stop. "Let's get off."

Before he could dismount and help her, Emily turned her back to the horse, protecting the baby, and slid to the ground with a soft thump. Mason didn't even wake up.

Levi dropped the reins and ground-tied Freckles as a red bird flew from one tree to the next. Emily stilled, watching, until the cardinal disappeared in the leaves. Overhead, but invisible, a warbler sang his courting song.

Courting, an old-fashioned word for what Levi was feeling in his heart. Emily deserved so much more than a broken-down cowboy who'd done nothing but cause her trouble. He had no right to court her.

What have you been doing for the last month?

The voice in his head was back.

He and Emily had grown close again. He loved being with her. He loved kissing her and listening to her laugh and watching her with Mason. Was that courting?

He hoped not. He couldn't. He had to be in Texas by the end of the month, and the last thing he wanted to do was upset Emily again.

"Want me to carry the papoose for a while?"

She shook her head. "I like holding him."

He heard what she didn't say. She liked holding him while she could, while baby and Levi were still here in Calypso.

His chest grew heavy, as if he'd swallowed a boulder. He should tell Emily that he was leaving soon.

She perched on the edge of the big rock next to the creek, swishing a hand back and forth in the clear water. Levi sat next to her. He smelled her perfume, spicy and fresh, like Emily.

She turned her head toward him and smiled. Everything inside Levi reached for her, leaned toward her, yearned for her.

Pivoting slightly, he cupped her jaw with one hand and stared into her green eyes, wishing he could stay right here with Emily forever.

She'd had a rough afternoon. Today was not a good day for goodbyes.

EMILY WATCHED emotions move across Levi's handsome face. Worry. Tenderness. Caring.

Bold as a red dress, she leaned forward and kissed him. Then just as quick, she stood and walked to the water's edge.

"Tadpoles. Hundreds of them."

Levi was silent for a beat before he answered. "Remember the time we caught a jar full, and you took them to science class? Mr. Black was cool like that."

"Then one morning we found tiny frogs hopping all over the classroom." She turned her head, holding him with her quiet gaze. "See? Not everything about this ranch was bad."

LEVI BLINKED AND GLANCED AWAY, but not before Emily saw the doubt on his face. She'd prayed and prayed that he would let go of his bitterness toward his father and stop dwelling on the hurtful incident that happened a long time ago. It hadn't been pleasant, but she hadn't let it destroy her.

Sometimes, she thought Levi had.

The truth she'd faced was plain and simple. She loved Levi, and every day with him, she loved him deeper. A woman's love for a man, not a girl's love for her teenage boyfriend.

She didn't want him to sell the ranch and move to Texas or anywhere else. Mason was part of the reason, but not the only one.

"This is a great place to raise a little boy." Emily kept her tone light, but she heard the hope hiding behind her words.

"No, it wasn't."

"It should have been. The ranch didn't make your childhood miserable, Levi. The owner did."

Expression going stern, he held up a hand. "Don't."

They'd never spoken of his father and what had happened. Yet the issue was there, between them every second, hovering like a stench that Levi refused to excise. "It's been fourteen years. We're adults now, not overreacting kids. We should be able to discuss the past and deal with it."

"Let it go, Emily."

Frustrated, she charged toward him. "That's exactly what you should do. *Let it go.* Forgive your dad. Deal with what happened, and forget about it."

Bitterly, he glared at her. "Have you?"

"Yes, until—"

He tilted away, knowing in his eyes. "Until I came back and dredged up everything."

Yes. And no. "All the more reason to get it out into the open, discuss it, and let it go. What your father did was reprehensible—"

"I said stop!" He spun away. At his loud voice, the horses jerked their heads up.

"Levi!"

He stalked to Freckles, mounted, and rode out of the woods, leaving her behind.

Again.

She grabbed Goldie's reins, but before she could figure out how to mount with a baby around her neck, Levi and his horse reappeared. He leaped to the ground, stalked toward her, and said, "I'm as big as jerk as Arlo Beech."

Emily opened her mouth to respond just as the cowboy yanked her as close as possible with Mason between them and kissed her with so much passion and emotion, her knees buckled.

There was desperation in his kisses, and unless she had lost her reason completely, a sweet hunger that said he cared. Maybe more than cared.

When he lifted his head, breathing like a dragon, she glared at him. "Are you finished?"

His nostrils flared. "No."

"Good. Me either." She pulled his face down and kissed him with all the love he didn't want her to feel.

13

Inside the living room of the Triple C's main house, Emily toed off her heels and propped bare feet on the leather ottoman. She was tired. Already today, she'd attended a Chamber of Commerce luncheon sandwiched in between work and plans for the town's summer festival, which included a rodeo at the Triple C, a softball tournament, and her new sister-in-law's petting farm.

All that effort meant Emily was overwhelmed. Toss in the problem with Levi and Mason, and she was fried.

At the moment, she had less than an hour to relax before her next appointment.

Last night, she'd barely slept. When she had, her dreams had been of Levi driving away, Mason waving from the back window, and a horse trailer filled with Jessica's clothes hooked behind the pick-up truck. Though the dream was distorted, she wondered if it was also prophetic.

"I've set myself up for heartache, Connie." She

moaned as she accepted a glass of sweet tea from her surrogate mother. "How could I be so dumb? I knew better. I even tried not to get involved."

Try didn't cut it when it came to Jessica's baby and the baby's uncle. They'd woven themselves around her heart until she was captured.

"You talk of Levi and Mason. No?" Connie's question held not a bit of surprise.

Emily nodded, miserable and confused.

Connie's dark fingers smoothed the top of Emily's hair, comforting as she'd always done. "This was my concern for you from the beginning. Your heart is tender and big, always open. You love so well."

Emily tilted her head to look into the other woman's loving face, grateful Connie hadn't said, "I told you so."

"But I promised not to let him affect me this time."

"Love does not listen to our directions, *mija*." Connie took the chair across from Emily and set her glass on the dark walnut coffee table with a soft click. "And you love him, *si*?"

"Oh, Connie. I do. In a different way than before and in a different way than I loved Dennis, but I do. The thought of losing him again is unbearable. He needs me, and so does Mason. And I need him. We're good together."

"You have told him this?"

"Not in so many words, but surely he knows I wouldn't be there if I didn't care." She certainly wouldn't have involved herself in a romantic relationship.

"And you believe Levi has no feelings of love for you?"

"I think he does, but he holds back." If his incredible

tenderness and desperate kisses were any indication, the man was crazy about her. "He's blinded by so much bitterness against his father that he can't see all the goodness right in front of his eyes. Even if he loves me, he won't let himself believe it. He certainly won't say it."

"And why is this, you think?"

Regret. Shame. Emily had never told another soul about that day, and she wouldn't now. Levi had suffered enough because of it. So had she.

Pretending ignorance, she hitched her shoulders and sipped her sweet drink.

"Then I will tell you, *mija*. Levi endured a harsh, crushing childhood. To keep Slim Donley from destroying his very soul, Levi buried his emotions deep. In here." Connie patted the flat of her hand against her chest. "Now he can't get them out."

"I agree, but at some point, he needs to get over all that. It's the past. His father is long dead." She hooked a lock of hair over one ear and sighed, frustrated. "He'll never be content anywhere until he does, but I don't know what to do to make him see that."

"When he first arrived, I feared for this, to see my Emily sad again because of this boy. But I watch him. Your brothers, they watch, too. People at church talk. Everyone sees how hard that man tries with Mason and the endless effort he has put into the ranch. Most of all, we see that Levi Donley is in love with our Emily, even if he doesn't know it." Connie sat on the couch and took Emily's hand in her warm, brown one. "We will pray about this. God and patience will make the difference."

Clinging to the hope that Connie was right, Emily

closed her eyes and prayed. Patience had to happen fast, or Levi would already be gone.

Two days.

Two whole days and nights since he'd seen Emily. Two days since her orange SUV had whipped into the driveway and made him glad all over. He missed her.

But being apart was good. It was right. It was for the best. They should not see each other. Not after the way he'd kissed her, the way she'd kissed him back. Not after the way she'd looked at him like a woman in love, demanding that he love her too.

He did. He always had.

But being apart was the most loving thing he could do for her. Not only because he couldn't go on loving her without saying something and making things worse. Last night had convinced him. He'd had the rotten dream about his father, only this time, Emily was trapped in the barn, and the old man blocked the doorway, laughing gleefully.

Only it hadn't been a dream. Not completely. Some ghosts wouldn't stay buried.

Levi had awakened with the awful sense of shame and humiliation and the knowledge that Texas was the best place for him and Mason. Anywhere away from Emily.

For all her bravado and insistence that they "discuss" the past, the truth was too hurtful. Every moment he was in her company reminded her of that day. Every moment they were together hurt her. Even if she denied it, Levi was convinced it was true. The sooner he was gone, the sooner she could forget him and his father. Again.

But today wasn't about him and his regrets. Today, Mason needed her.

What was he supposed to do about that?

Levi paced the hardwood floor and bounced Mason against his shoulder. Mason wailed. Face red and distorted with crying, the baby had been unhappy all day. Levi had tried everything he knew. The problem was, he knew so little.

Emily would know what was wrong. She could make it better.

He paced into the living room and stared up at his brother's photo. "What do I do, bro?"

You know what to do. Pray. Call Emily. Forgive.

The voice in his head had been talking a lot lately. Aunt Ruby said it was the Holy Spirit, Who knew all things.

"If you really know everything, I wish you'd let me in on the big picture."

If I did, you'd freak out. A little light's all you need.

Levi snorted. Did God use terms like *freak out*?

Holding the baby to him with one hand, he whispered a short prayer. Nothing magic happened, so he reached for his cell phone.

He shot off a text to Emily.

Ten minutes later, she still hadn't replied, so he shot off another. This time he told the truth. *Something's wrong with Mason.* He hated to do that to her, but otherwise, she would go on ignoring him.

His cell phone rang. If Mason hadn't been screaming in his ear, he would have grinned.

He answered. "Hello."

"What's wrong?"

"Mason won't stop crying."

"Is he hungry? Wet? Sleepy?"

Levi frowned and answered the rapid-fire questions in the order they were asked. "He wouldn't take his bottle. He has a dry diaper. And he won't go to sleep. He just screams in my ear."

"Does he have fever?"

Fever? Why hadn't he thought of that? "I don't know."

Mason quieted momentarily, and Levi sagged against the wall. Ah, the sweet sound of silence.

It was short-lived, apparently only a nanosecond for the baby to catch his breath and crank into overdrive.

"The thermometer is in the nursery in the top drawer."

He knew that. He started up the stairs. "Will you come over?"

She hesitated. He could feel it, hear it in the soft indrawn breath. She didn't want to see him. Levi thought his heart would crack like the Liberty Bell.

Stupid reaction. He didn't want her to want to see him. Right?

"Mason's better when you rock him. I think he misses you. Come. Please." Mason missed her. Levi missed her. He'd be lying to say different.

"I'm in Rock Springs. The drive will take at least forty-five minutes."

Rock Springs? That was a world away. Why was she there?

And why was he being so unfair?

"We'll wait." Stupid thing to say. What else was he going to do?

"Put the phone up to his ear."

"What? Why?"

"Just do it, Levi. Or put me on speaker."

Speaker. He could do that and bounce a crying baby at the same time.

He pushed the proper button, balanced the phone on the windowsill, and stared out at the green pasture below the nursery. Mason had been fussy all day, so Levi had not done a single bit of ranch work. None. He'd barely fed Butter who, even now, trotted into the nursery behind him, golden canine eyes looking from Levi to Mason with worry.

Yes, he'd let the dog inside. It was that or listen to him whine and scratch at the door because his baby was crying.

Emily's voice came through the speaker. Soft, sweet, pure. She was singing.

Levi's insides squeezed. He melted like a Hershey bar on the dashboard in mid-July. Grabbing the phone, he carried it and the baby to the padded rocker where he leaned his head back against the cushions and closed his eyes.

Emily's warm soprano wafted over him. His shoulders relaxed. He took a deep breath, and let it go, slow and easy.

Mason's crying eased the slightest bit. He paused as

if listening. But then, he cranked right up again. Had the baby recognized Emily's voice? Had he bonded to her?

Of course, he had. And now, Levi would separate them forever, the way his father had separated him from his mother.

But Emily wasn't Mason's mother.

Tell that to Mason.

God, I don't know what you want me to do.

Give it to me. Let me carry it.

Give you what?

Emily changed songs. The baby's wails slowed to an occasional outburst and finally to fussy whimpers.

The little man shuddered a long sigh. Levi let out one of his own. Relief, even if only for a few minutes.

The magic of Emily.

EMILY DROVE at the top of the speed limit, singing a mix of Spanish and English lullabies and hymns for forty-five minutes over her car's Bluetooth speaker. When she finally pulled up to Levi's ranch, all was quiet on the other end of the phone. After parking the car, she sat for a couple of minutes, considering whether to enter the house or not. The baby wasn't crying. Levi wasn't speaking. They must be mercifully asleep. Maybe she should turn around and go home.

Patience, Connie had said. Patience and prayer. She'd done a lot of praying since that day by the creek.

She started the car and pulled the gear into drive.

The front door opened, and Levi stepped out in sock

feet, his hair sticking up and a day's worth of scruff on his face.

Emily turned to mush.

She killed the engine and got out. What else could she do when the man looked this wrecked?

"Rough day?" she teased as she joined him on the porch.

"And night." He scrubbed at the top of his head. "Thanks for singing. That's the longest he's been anywhere close to calm all day. He's asleep now."

"Poor baby." She patted Levi's shoulder. "You and him both. But if his temperature is normal and he's not crying, it looks like my job here is done. I'll head home."

She turned to leave.

Strong fingers clasped her upper arm. "No. Don't go. Not yet."

Emily turned back and gave him a long, cool look. She should leave. Get away while she still had a brain cell left.

Levi winced. "He might wake up."

"You could call me again, and I'll sing to him."

His shoulders drooped. He scrubbed the top of his head again and blew out a breath. Brown eyes begged her.

"Stay. Please."

"Admit you want me to stay for you, not just for Mason, and I'll think about it."

"You know I do."

She started to push harder, to ask him to admit he loved her, but Connie's word of the week flashed in her head. *Patience.*

"For a little while, then. I have paperwork to do."

"You always have paperwork."

True, she did, but she needed the excuse to leave if her emotions became overwhelmed.

"You can do it here. I won't bother you. I'll flop on the couch, hope and pray Mason stays asleep, and watch you work."

"You really are desperate."

"You have no idea."

She gave him a cryptic smile. This kind of desperate was good for him. "Yes, I do."

He led the way into the house, and like always, she was struck by Jessica's presence—in the furnishings, the colors, the photos on the wall. Would Levi leave all these things behind? Or take them with him to Texas?

"Want some coffee?"

"No, thanks. It's nearly dinnertime. I'm getting hungry. What have you eaten today?"

He screwed his face up really cute. "I don't remember."

"What's in the fridge to cook?"

"Some burger meat, smoked sausage, bacon, eggs. Are you fixing supper?"

She pointed toward the couch. "Go. Nap. I'll look in on the baby and figure out something for us to eat."

He didn't argue. He flopped onto the couch with the loudest sigh she'd ever heard, crossed his arms over his chest, and closed his eyes.

Emily tiptoed up the stairs and found Butter sprawled next to the baby crib, his nose on his paws. Big golden eyes watched her enter. The tail swished back and forth on the area rug in welcome.

She dragged a hand over the yellow head and peered over the crib railing. Mason lay sprawled with all four limbs flopped outward in exhaustion. Emily touched a hand to his forehead. Still no fever. Must have been colic or an upset tummy or a dozen other reasons babies don't feel well but can't talk about it. She whispered a prayer that the worst was over.

When he didn't stir or cry out, she tiptoed back to the kitchen and found the ingredients for spaghetti and meatballs. There wasn't a green leafy vegetable anywhere to be found, so she opened a can of green beans and put three slices of bread in the toaster. Buttered and sprinkled with garlic powder, the toast should pass for garlic bread.

When the simple meal was ready, she went into the living room to wake the cowboy. Like his exhausted nephew, he was totally out. One arm hung over the couch and touched the floor. His brown lashes swept his cheekbones, and his lips were slightly parted.

Unable, or unwilling, to resist, Emily leaned down and kissed him.

Instantly, Levi's eyes popped open. His mouth curved. "Supper ready?"

"Unless you want to sleep longer."

He reached for her hands and tugged her down to sit on the edge of the couch next to him. "Do that again."

"What? This?" She leaned in and kissed him.

He gave a happy, humming sigh. "Oh, yeah. Best

wake-up ever. But I'm not quite alert yet. Better do it again."

Emily snickered at his playfulness but smacked his lips with hers, quick and loud, before starting to move away.

His arm looped around her shoulders and held her close to his chest. "Don't go."

"The toast is getting cold."

"It's only bread. I'd rather live on love."

The word love startled her, froze her in place. Maybe it shocked him too because he quieted, his gaze holding hers.

"Love is a gift from God, Levi."

He swallowed but said nothing. His eyes were soft and yearning, but he couldn't get the words out.

So she did it for him. "I love you."

He let his arm fall to the side. "Don't."

"Too late."

He sighed and glanced away. "I'm sorry."

Emily leaned back but stayed close, a hand on his chest.

Drawing on Connie's insight that Levi's childhood had pushed his emotions down deep, she persisted. "I think you love me, too, but you're too scared or stubborn or stupid to admit it."

"All the above." He dropped his feet to the floor and sat up, pinning her with a beseeching gaze. "I'm not good for you, Em. You deserve better. You were always a cut above the Donleys. Still are."

The broken boy had become a broken man. And rescuer Emily wanted to help him heal.

She touched his jaw, caressing the whiskery skin, feeling tender and every bit as scared as he was, but if he left without knowing how much she cared, she'd always wonder what might have been. And he'd never let go of the past and heal.

"Would you let me decide what I do or don't deserve? And for once in your life, let someone love you without feeling guilty or responsible or whatever issue you're having. Can't we just be Emily and Levi and forget the rest?"

He was quiet for another moment while Emily summoned all her patience and hope and prayed for God to touch the place in Levi that needed Him so desperately.

She needed him too. For too long, her emotions had been on hold. Now she understood what she'd been waiting for.

Levi sighed. Then he cupped the back of her head and pulled her close. As he kissed her, he murmured, "Is this dessert or the main course? I'm really hungry."

Emily jerked away. "Levi!" She whacked his shoulder and stood. "Can't you be serious?"

"I'm teasing you, Em." Levi followed her up and reeled her back in. As he rocked her against his cowboy body, all the levity disappeared. "You've always had my heart. Always."

And for now, that was enough for Emily.

14

L evi whistled, and the yellow dog bounded around the corner of the barn and came to a skidding halt next to Mason's stroller.

"Where you been, boy? Chasing rabbits? We got work to do."

The dog's tail thumped like mad. He smiled his doggie grin, eyes dancing with delight in his master. In the days and weeks since he'd strayed onto the Donley Ranch, Butter had filled out, and his dull yellow coat had turned to gold. He was a handsome cuss.

Even Nate thought so. He'd said as much when he'd stopped by, at his sister's request, to check the dog over and vaccinate him. Even though Nate wasn't a vet, he was the closest thing Calypso had, and he was mighty good at it. Emily wanted to be sure Butter was healthy, since he'd taken such an interest in Mason. Fine with Levi. He wanted that too.

"Be useful now. Lay down there by the stroller and keep an eye on our boy. I got hooves to clean and file."

The barn lot held half a dozen horses he and Freckles had rounded up at daylight. All six needed some foot work.

With the baby in clear sight but out of reach of the horses, Levi slipped through the gate and got busy.

The sun was hot on his back, a harbinger of a warm summer on the way. But the flats of Texas would be hotter. Might as well get acclimated.

He'd talked to Jack Parnell on the phone this morning and reiterated his plan to be on The Long Spur by the end of the month. Less than two weeks.

With Freckles's foot trapped between his knees, he picked away at the debris under the frog, the foot's v-shaped cushion.

Funny how he'd been so excited about the Texas job, but now he dreaded it.

He paused to tip his hat back and take a closer look at the hoof.

Emily was the problem. She loved him. He'd suspected it for a while, but he'd tried to pretend not to. It was easier to make decisions that way. He'd rather take a nosedive off a bucking horse that see her hurt, but she didn't understand. He was trying to do what was best for her as well as himself. She didn't need the likes of him messing up her life.

The question was, why would Emily love him? Why would she even be willing to look at him?

Because she has a big, forgiving heart.

Yeah. That was his Em. Loving and good. Saint Emily.

He wondered if she'd ever consider moving away from Calypso.

Nah, she was happy here. Her family was here, and their relationships were close and binding. Not like his. She had roots. Her life, her church, her job, her friends were here. He couldn't ask her to move to Texas with him.

You could stay.

Levi ignored the voice and reached for a file to smooth a jagged edge on Freckles's hoof. Two fingers to the pastern told him the pulse was strong.

He glanced up to check on Mason. Whatever had caused the twenty-four-hour crying jag was mercifully over. The baby was eating and happy today.

Was it because of Emily? Had her presence and her sweet singing soothed something inside an infant who might be missing his mother?

The thought haunted him—that Mason would grieve and ache for a woman's touch.

He'd hire a female caregiver in Texas.

But she wouldn't be Emily.

He completed cleaning Freckle's hooves and turned him out to pasture. As he led Goldie, the palomino, into the lot for her turn, a car turned down the driveway. Dust stirred up behind in small puffs instead of billowing clouds, a testament to the good spring rains they'd had.

Spring rains that had killed his brother.

Sometimes he'd go for hours, even a whole day, without remembering, and then the heartache would sweep over him in a massive wave. A tsunami. Like now. He wanted to ignore the car, sit down on the ground, stick his face in his hat, and wail as loud as Mason had. That's how bad his chest ached.

The car stopped at the end of the drive. Levi left Goldie in the lot and went to greet the visitor, pushing the stroller in front of him. Mason made happy noises and waved his arms at the toys dangling from the handle. Butter trailed alongside.

Levi squinted into the sun. He didn't recognize the vehicle, but with the ranch up for sale, he figured he'd start seeing some traffic soon. Anyway, he hoped he did. He had two weeks to sell or do this thing long distance.

A slim, fortyish woman in black slacks and a pink top exited the driver's side, lifted a hand to shade her eyes, and watched his approach. A man stayed in the passenger's seat but had turned to gaze around the property.

"Is this the Donley Ranch?" she asked as Levi approached.

His hopes lifted. Definitely a house hunter. "Yes, ma'am. I'm Levi Donley."

The woman stepped close to the stroller and peered inside. She softened the way he'd seen dozens of women do when they looked at the baby. In church, at the store, it didn't matter. Mason had admirers. Every single time, Levi puffed up with pride. The little man was something special.

"This must be the orphaned Donley baby," she said. "What's his name?"

"Mason."

She reached inside the stroller. "Mind if I hold him?"

Levi frowned. This was more than casual interest, and

he didn't like the idea of a stranger handling his boy. He put a hand on Mason's chest, stopping her.

"I'd rather you didn't. Are you here to look at the house? The realtor didn't mention an appointment, but I could have missed her call."

The woman drew back, eyebrows drawn together in question. "The house? No, we're here for the baby. We drove all the way from Nebraska to get him."

Hair rose on the back of Levi's neck. "What are you talking about?"

Seemingly determined to have her hands on Mason, she chucked the baby under the chin. "When we got the call from Child Services, I was shocked. We had no idea Marilyn had two sons in Oklahoma. And now a grandchild."

Levi's ears began to ring. Marilyn? His mother?

"Ma'am, I don't know you, and I don't know what you're talking about. My mother hasn't been in my life since I was a toddler."

"I'm Rosanna Tompkins." She said the name as if he should recognize it. He didn't.

When he didn't respond, she tried again. "My husband was related to your mother, and when we learned about the orphaned baby, we felt it was our duty to step up and take him in."

"Take him in? You mean, take custody of him?" Was that what she was trying to say? She wanted his boy?

Levi began to shake his head and slowly pull the stroller away from the woman. This wasn't happening. "I don't know where you got your information, but Mason is not available."

"We spoke to a social worker. She was searching for relatives. At first, we didn't understand any of this either. We barely knew Marilyn and never knew you boys. But after considerable thought, we decided taking him as our own was the right thing to do."

Levi's stomach sank all the way to the green grass.

Emily. Had Emily sent this woman?

He swallowed the bile that rose in this throat as bitter as his mood. "I don't care who you spoke to. You're not taking Mason anywhere."

Mrs. Tompkins's face tightened. She made another move toward Mason.

Levi stepped around the stroller and blocked her view. Butter scooted in at the side as if he, too, was feeling the negative vibes.

A sense of protectiveness more fierce than anything he'd ever experienced rushed over Levi. He'd fight for this boy. He'd stop anyone who tried to take him. Even Emily. No matter what he had to do.

Through tight teeth, he ground, "Don't touch him. He's *my* son."

The word ballooned in his mind. *Son.* Mason was his child.

"That was not my understanding."

"Then your understanding was wrong." Now, go, leave, and don't come back.

"We've already spoken to an attorney. We're filing for custody."

Levi's stomach lurched into his throat. He thought he might choke. Or throw up. "Not going to happen."

He'd run if he had to, but no one was taking this baby.

The woman pulled herself up straight and tall. With a huff, she said, "We'll see about that. I didn't drive all this way to go home empty-handed."

Then she spun away, marched to her car, and slammed the door hard enough to rattle the countryside.

As the vehicle sped down the drive, stirring far more dust this time, Levi watched in dismay, his disappointment bitter.

Emily had done this to him. Emily. The woman who claimed to love him. The woman he loved.

She had never wanted him to raise Mason. She'd been against him from the start.

But she'd changed her mind. Hadn't she?

Wrong again, cowboy. Sweet Emily sabotaged you.

She must have gone right on searching for another relative to adopt Mason even after she'd learned of Levi's decision. Why would she do that? And why would she say she loved him and then stab him in the back?

He tilted his head and stared up at the marshmallow clouds, finding no answers except betrayal.

EMILY HUMMED as she hoed around the edge of her front flowerbed. Last night with Levi had been wonderful, even if she'd left early so he could get some much-needed sleep. The two hours they'd been together had been like old times. Better than old times. They were adults now, mature and sensible. One ugly, embarrassing incident would no longer come between them, and someday soon, Levi would release his long-held animosity towards his father and find the peace he needed.

She believed that with all her heart. Just as she knew she loved him enough to leave Calypso if he asked.

The decision hadn't been easy, but she wanted him and Mason to be her future, wherever that took them. He'd hinted a few times last night, discussing the Texas job, the manager's house that was big enough for a family, and his desire to settle down with a wife and kids pretty soon. He already had the kid, he'd joked. Now, he needed the wife.

That was Levi's way. Dance around the subject until he could get the words out. If he broached the topic again tonight, Emily was ready with her answer.

From a flat of started flowers, she removed a little pink pansy plant and stuck it in the prepared hole. An entire bed of these would add cheerful color until late fall.

A car door slammed behind her, not unusual with her brothers and Connie and the ranch hands of the Triple C swirling all over the big ranch all day long. Her house was an easy stop for iced tea or a bathroom break. She pivoted on her toes with a greeting on her lips.

Levi stormed across the lawn, looking angrier than a thundercloud.

Her heart dropped. "Is Mason sick again?"

"No." The word was terse and sharp.

The baby was okay. He must be in the truck. But something was most definitely amiss.

Emily stood and dusted her gloved hands together. "What's wrong?"

"You. How could you do this to me? To us?"

She blinked, confused. So much for running to him with arms open. "What are you talking about?"

"I had a rather unpleasant visit from some woman and man who claim to be long lost relatives of mine. And Mason's." He slammed his hands onto his hips. "I have no idea who they are, but guess what they want?"

She lifted her shoulders, wary. Wasn't finding lost family a good thing? From Levi's mood, she didn't think so. At least not to him. "To get to know you? To invite you to a family reunion?"

His eyes narrowed. His nostrils flared. "They want Mason."

Oh, no. Not now. Emily licked suddenly dry lips. "Who are they?"

"You know who they are. You sent them. The Tompkinses." He jabbed a finger at her. "You never wanted me to adopt Mason. From the start, you wanted someone else —anyone else—and set up some kind of search for other relatives."

Fighting the temptation to slap away that pointing finger, Emily took a deep breath. Calm and reasonable. The way she talked to angry clients. "Yes, that's part of my job, but—"

"Did you talk to them today? Did you send them to my ranch?"

"No! Levi, listen to me." So much for calm and reasonable. "I don't even know who these people are. No one contacted me."

"Then how did they find me? I'll tell you how. You. You sent them, expecting me to hand over my nephew after you led me to believe I was doing okay as his dad."

His voice was wounded, desperate. "Was it because I had one rough day when I didn't know why he was crying? Is that it? You declared me unfit because Mason cried, and I called you for help?"

"No, no. Levi, no." She put a hand on his arm.

He shook her off.

"I had nothing to do with this. At least not today. Get Mason out of the truck and come in the house. Let's sit down and discuss this like adults."

"What's to discuss? The Tompkins woman said they'd already filed for custody. They're taking me to court to fight for Mason."

"They won't win. You're his uncle, a closer relative. And I promise you, I do not know who these people are. I didn't send them."

"Then how did they find my house? How did they know Mason is—was—an orphan?"

"I don't know. You have to believe me."

"But you searched for other relatives. Somebody besides me. You thought I was the wrong choice. Didn't you?"

"That was two months ago before I knew you again. Before I saw how good you are with Mason." *Back when I was afraid of loving you.*

A strange expression crossed his face. A realization.

A slow hiss slid through his teeth. "Finding that couple wasn't about Mason at all, was it?"

"Levi, you're not making any sense."

"This was about me." He jabbed a finger against his chest. "About my old man. It took fourteen years, but keeping Mason away from me is payback."

A cold chill ran down Emily's spine. She stiffened. "Payback? You actually think I'd do something like that?"

"What else am I to think? The moment I let down my guard and admit I'm still crazy about you, this happens. Feels like revenge to me."

"That's the dumbest thing I've ever heard!" Hurt turned to anger. The man had lost his mind.

"I should have run with Mason the moment I got him."

"Run, then, Levi. That's what you do best." Emily started to shake. She was so mad, her eyeballs were on fire. "When life gets hard, you run. The problem is, you'll never be happy until you stop running and let go of what your father did. I love you, you idiotic cowboy, but that's never been enough. Not then. Not now. So go away, and don't come back."

Furiously, she threw her gloves at him. He caught them, stared at her for two beats, and then spun on his boot heels and left the same way he'd arrived. Furious.

HE WAS DONE. Finished. Through. And if a breaking heart made noise, his would be a sonic boom.

Levi lifted Mason from the car seat and held him close. "No worries, champ. Me and you, we're a team. Nobody's going to separate us."

He didn't want to accept the truth, but the evidence had driven right up to his door. Emily had found someone else to adopt Mason, another relative, someone with a legal means to fight his claim. Levi Donley hadn't been good enough.

Hadn't he known that all along? Hadn't he tried to tell her from the start? And yet Scott had chosen him, and he hadn't been able to abandon his brother's son or deny his brother's last wish. He loved Mason, and he was trying his best to be a good dad. Didn't that count for anything?

Apparently not to Emily.

Then why did she say she loved you?

"Good question." Levi shook his head. He was in no mood to deal with the voice.

He placed the baby on the couch for a diaper change. "Love you, buddy."

There. He'd said the words out loud. And he planned to say them a lot over the next hundred years. A kid needed that. He'd needed that and never gotten it.

He had a feeling Scott and Jessica had said the words a million times. Maybe that's why his childhood home felt different now. Love had chased the meanness away.

Diaper tabs sealed without so much as sticking them to his thumbs, Levi cleaned his hands and lifted Mason up to look at the photos on the wall.

"That's your daddy and mama. They love you too. Only they have to love you from heaven. Someday, I'll tell you all about them."

Except he couldn't tell Mason about Jessica. He hadn't known her.

Emily was her best friend.

Emily wouldn't be around. He and Mason were headed for Texas. Two days, tops. As soon as he could pack and tie up loose ends. The realtor could handle the ranch sale.

This time, he wouldn't be back. He'd never see this place again. He'd never see Emily again either.

That was the kicker. Even after what she'd done, he didn't want to leave her. He still loved her. But then, he'd always loved Emily Caldwell.

Now that his temper had cooled, he wanted to talk to her. He shouldn't have attacked without listening. He didn't know what had come over him.

Yes, he did. Betrayal. Fear that she didn't really love him, that she couldn't, that no one ever would. So, he'd driven her away.

If he loved her, let her go. Wasn't that the old adage?

Some things just weren't meant to be. A relationship between him and Emily was one of them.

15

Emily spent the next morning at the office trying to sort out the mess with the Tompkins couple. Levi was right about one thing. This was her fault.

He was wrong, however, on every other account. If he hadn't been so livid, the idea of her taking revenge against him for an incident that had happened fourteen years would have been laughable. But today, she was not laughing about anything.

Headache, throat tight, chest about to crack open, Emily hurt all over. She'd even considered staying home from work with her head buried in the pillow. Instead, she'd forced herself to get up and spend extra time in prayer. Though God hadn't sent any direct answers, He'd calmed her soul.

The trouble was, the moment she'd gotten to work, peace fled, and one problem after another moved in. A court case she'd worked on for months was canceled. A noncustodial dad had bolted with his toddler, and she'd sent out an Amber Alert. Then an irate parent stormed the office demanding her children back, even though the woman had left them alone for three days. The oldest was seven.

She rubbed the throbbing spot between her eyes. As if all those issues weren't enough, a foster parent had called asking that the children in her care be removed.

And then there were the Tompkinses.

"I'd given up on finding anyone except Levi," she told her boss when he came into her cubicle with a fresh stack of file folders. Her case load grew heavier by the second.

"The Tompkins couple didn't make contact with you before this?"

"No. In fact, I'd forgotten about them. We spoke months ago, and only briefly. They claimed to have no knowledge of a Scott Donley or any relatives in Oklahoma, so I eliminated them and moved on."

"Then what's the deal? Why are they in Calypso now?"

"Good question. Denise spoke to them on the phone yesterday when I was out of the office, but she told them the situation was already resolved."

"Then how did they find their way to the Donley Ranch?"

"GPS? Google?" She tossed her hands up and moaned. "I don't know. Calypso is a small town. They could have asked anywhere and gotten directions."

"Don't let it get to you, Emily. Stuff happens, and these things usually work themselves out. No judge is going to give them custody if the uncle is a fit parent."

"He is, and I'm confident the judge will agree. It's just that the situation has caused a lot of grief for Mr. Donley." And for her.

"Probably for the Tompkinses, too. They've come a considerable distance."

She hadn't even considered the couple's feelings. "I have a meeting scheduled with them."

"Good. Explain the situation and assure them the baby is being well cared for. Apologize for their inconvenience, see if Levi will let them visit the baby in his presence, and try to convince them to drop their suit."

She pulled a wry face. "You give me all the easy assignments."

With a grin, he tapped his knuckles on her desk and started out of the cubicle but immediately turned back. "One other thing to add to your easy list. Got a call from Calypso School on Daisy Beech again. Take a drive out there after you see the Tompkinses and talk to the dad. She's only been in school one day this week."

"Oh, boy." A confrontation with Arlo Beech would just about cap her rotten day. "We're going to have to turn him over to the DA if this isn't resolved soon."

"Tell him that. A fine sometimes wakes people up."

"News like that should go over well."

Tim left, and Emily gathered her things to meet with Mr. and Mrs. Tompkins. Her relationship with Levi was over, but she could right this wrong and leave him and Mason in peace.

The headache pounded harder as she drove the distance to Calypso and to the meeting with Mason's long-lost relatives. From what she could determine, they were distant relatives, cousins of Levi's mother. No one knew where Marilyn Donley was or if she was even still alive. But no one blamed the woman for disappearing either, though everyone wondered why she'd left her sons with Slim Donley. The man was that awful.

She shuddered to remember the mean-spirited rancher who'd made Scott and Levi miserable as boys. The man who'd trapped her in the barn. She'd avoided him most of the time, but that day had been different. She'd thought Slim and Scott were out of town for a cow sale. She'd thought Levi would be alone.

She'd been wrong.

Emily turned up the radio to drown out the memories. She'd forgiven and moved on. A revisit to that ugly moment when Levi stepped inside that stall, his face ashen and horrified, served no good purpose.

They'd been teenagers, unable to handle that kind of fright and humiliation, unable to discuss what had happened so they could put it behind them.

The incident had scarred Levi, and because of his reaction, had changed the trajectory of their entire lives. Even now, so many years later, Levi was trapped in his father's meanness.

She'd thought he was healing. She'd believed Scott's death would open his eyes. She'd trusted that love would bring them back together.

She'd been wrong about that too. Maybe the time had come to give up on Levi Donley and let him go.

Heart heavy, head throbbing, she pulled into the lot of Calypso's only hotel and parked.

Regardless of her personal feelings, she had a job to

do. Rosanna and Doug Tompkins had no chance of gaining custody of Mason, and they needed to know. They also deserved to know that Levi was a good parent, a perfect match for Mason, and that he loved the little boy with everything he had.

As she well knew, Levi kept a lot of love locked up inside him. He'd only begun to let it out.

An hour and a half later, she left the hotel and headed toward Daisy's home. The fact that she had to drive past Levi's ranch to get there was not lost on her. As she sailed past, she couldn't help but glance toward his house. His truck was in the driveway, but she didn't spot Levi or the dog.

Foolish, but she'd wanted a glimpse.

He wouldn't want to see her, though, even to learn how the Tompkins's meeting had gone. She'd have to talk to him at some point but not today when her feelings were so terribly raw.

Next to the mailbox at the end of the driveway, stuck in the midst of Jessica's purple irises, a new sign had been erected. A real estate sign. *For Sale.*

Sorrow gripped her, squeezed her breath. Reality was here. Levi was really going to leave her again.

It was with her head muddled that she knocked on Arlo Beech's door and listened for the footsteps. Daisy should be here if she wasn't at school. When no one came, she walked around the corner to the back of the house and shielded her eyes toward the barn and the cow lots.

"What do you want?"

The voice came from behind. She whirled around.

Arlo Beech came toward her from behind a shed, his ever-present rifle swinging at his side.

When he recognized her, he stopped. His eyes narrowed in a hardened face. "I told you not to come here again."

The tone threatened. He cocked a hip in an intentionally belligerent stance.

The man was never happy to see her, but today, antagonism radiated from him in waves. His glare pierced her, a glassy-eyed, bloodshot glare, and his stance was unsteady. Had he been drinking?

Not good. But she'd faced belligerent, inebriated people before. Unfortunately.

Do the job and get out of here fast.

"Is Daisy home?"

"Around here somewhere. She's busy. Got work to do."

"I'd like to speak to her please. She missed school every day but once this week."

"So?" As though the idea of school was repugnant, he curled his lip. "She's learning all she needs right here."

"I'm afraid the law disagrees with you, sir." They'd had this discussion before. Beech knew the rules. He simply didn't want to comply. "Daisy needs to be back in school tomorrow and remain there consistently or her case will be turned over to the DA."

Scowling, Beech took one step in her direction.

"You threatening me?" Words slurred, he wobbled as he hefted the rifle waist high.

Emily retreated a step. The hair tingled the back of her neck.

"No, sir. I'm only stating facts." She kept her voice calm, though her insides shook. The man looked menacing. The rifle even more so. And he was definitely drunk.

Emily raised a palm as if to stop his advance and spoke softly, tone appeasing. "Please put the gun down, Mr. Beech. I mean no harm."

"No? You're coming around here all the time, stirring up my daughter, making her lazy. That's harm to me." He turned his head to the side and spat. "No busy-body social worker is going to tell me how to raise my own kid. Now git while you can."

Where was Daisy? Was she okay? Was she safe?

"I need to speak to Daisy before I leave."

The man hackled. He lurched forward. "You accusing me of something?"

Emily's blood pressure shot to the sky. She breathed a silent prayer.

"I need to see her." And make sure she's all right. She searched for a reason, any reason, to talk to the child. Before she found one, Beech took another, threatening step.

She backed away. The headache she'd fought all day blurred her thoughts.

"Like I said, you better leave." He raised the gun higher, holding the sight to his eye. "Git. Now!"

Emily's mouth went dry as cotton. She froze like a jackrabbit in the crosshairs.

If he didn't put that rifle down, something terrible might happen. "Please lower the gun. I'm only trying to help Daisy and keep you from receiving a fine or jail time."

"Jail? For raising my kid as I see fit?" He released a string of obscenities. His finger moved to the trigger.

Fight or flight kicked in. Emily was no match for an enraged man and a rifle. But Beech was between her and her vehicle. She moved to go around him. He blocked the way, shoved her back, and aimed the rifle straight for her chest.

LEVI THUMPED a cardboard box on a chair and began the painful task of clearing out Scott's dresser. Socks, T-shirts, a pair of boxers that made him laugh. Jessica must have gotten them for her husband. He put the items in the box and opened the next drawer.

At the bottom was a picture of the two brothers, him and Scott, standing next to an old red pick-up truck. Levi remembered that day like it happened yesterday. Scott was laughing. He'd always been laughing.

The old man had been in the hospital. A kidney stone. And the two Donley brothers were revved up and ready to hit the big town of Calypso with their girlfriends.

Emily had taken the picture.

He set the photo on top of the dresser. Mason would want that someday. In fact, he'd box up all the photos he could find to take with him. The same for a few of Scott's other things. His belt buckle. His rifle. His saddle and spurs. Maybe his hat too.

Tears clogged the back of his throat. Getting rid of Scott's belongings was harder than he'd expected.

Butter roamed in, sniffed the box and returned to the nursery where Mason was napping.

The baby needed to wake up soon, or he wouldn't sleep tonight. They had a nice routine going, he and the baby and the dog. Work in the mornings with Mason strapped to his chest or in the stroller. A break for lunch. More work in the afternoons and often until dark. Mason was an easy baby, happy unless he was hungry, sleepy, or wet, which made working the ranch a whole lot easier. Today, Levi had knocked off early to pack. The dressers should have been cleaned out before now, but Levi was dragging his feet, and he knew it. Never before had he minded leaving things behind and unsettled, but he did this time. *He* felt unsettled. Lonely. Empty.

Emily hadn't done anything wrong. He'd known that as soon as he'd calmed down. She hadn't intentionally sabotaged him. She'd been genuinely shocked.

He should call her, go see her, apologize.

Nah, dumb move. He and Mason were due in Texas. No use reopening old wounds. Better to move on and let her forget him.

Why was leaving so much harder than before?

Because you're wrong and old enough to know it this time.

Aunt Ruby's Holy Spirit again, nudging.

"I want to do right by her, God. Everything's so messed up." He folded a pair of pajama bottoms and put them in the box.

Jessica's dresser was yet to come, a task Emily had planned to do. A labor of love, she'd called it. He couldn't refuse her the right to sort through Jessica's belongings and keep whatever she wanted. It was only fair. But not now. Not when he was afraid seeing her would confuse him even more. Maybe he'd send a message for her to go through the closets and drawers after he and Mason were gone.

He cleared Scott's dresser, sorting as he went. Things he wanted to keep. Things for Mason. Things for the church clothes closet.

Every item pierced his heart. Besides Mason, these were all that was left of his brother. The idea of Scott being reduced to a stack of cardboard boxes made him want to weep.

Time for a break.

He bolted from the bedroom and rushed down the stairs as fast as he could without waking the baby.

He headed for the kitchen and gulped a glass of water. The liquid clogged his esophagus, painful and big as a fist.

He stepped out on the back porch, closed his eyes and breathed long and deep. Everything about this move felt wrong.

A loud *pop* jerked him around. What was that? A gunshot?

He peered out into the pasture. The sound seemed to have come from the direction of Beech's place. Was the hateful neighbor target-shooting with that rifle of his?

Levi continued to stare in that direction, troubled. The man was plain mean. Levi wouldn't put it past Beech to shoot Butter or one of the Donley cows or horses if it strayed onto his property.

Butter was safe upstairs. But what about his horses? Freckles grazed around the barn with Goldie, but the other four were nowhere to be seen.

He heard the pop again and started for the barn and

Freckles. The horse saw him coming and trotted to the fence. Levi opened the gate, intending to saddle up and ride when his brain clicked in. Mason was in the house. No way he'd take the baby along if some nut was shooting a rifle. Did he dare leave him in the crib? And if he did, would that be fodder for the Tompkinses to claim custody?

Before he could work things out in his brain, a blond head appeared on the horizon. Daisy raced toward him. As she drew nearer, she screamed his name.

Fear prickled the skin on his arms.

She screamed his name again.

Something was wrong. Very wrong.

Levi tossed a leg over Freckles's bare back and rode out to meet her.

Daisy was white as cotton and shaking like a leaf. She leaned forward, hands to knees, breathless.

He slid from the saddle to the ground next to her. "What's happened?"

"Miss Emily." She pointed back behind her. "Hurry."

His adrenaline jacked. "Where?"

"The field." The child started to sob. "She's hurt."

That's all Levi needed to hear. "Stay with Mason."

Fear pumped through his veins more powerful than hot lava as he leaned over Freckles's mane and let the cutting horse have his head. They crossed the forty acres in Derby time.

As they approached the fence, he saw Emily. Ten years of his life disappeared in one glance. She lay on the ground, still, quiet. He didn't know if she was dead or alive.

He also didn't know where Beech was, nor did he care. Emily was hurt. She needed him.

Sliding to the thick pasture grass, he fell down beside her. Blood stained her dress above the knee.

"Emily." He touched her face.

She didn't open her eyes.

"Baby, where are you hurt? Talk to me. Oh, God, please save her."

Emily didn't move.

Frantic, he slapped his pocket for his cell phone and called 9-1-1, directing them to the Donley Ranch. They'd never find her down in this field, but she couldn't ride either.

Carefully, calling her name, promising to take care of her, babbling his crazy mixed-up love, Levi slid her skirt a few inches above her knee. Her leg was a mess and bleeding badly. Profusely. He had no idea if she was hit anywhere else, and he was afraid to look.

Quickly, Levi removed his shirt and tied it around her thigh. Then, as gently as possible, he picked her up and ran toward his house.

16

The hospital corridor smelled like blood. The notion that it was Emily's blood made Levi weak in the knees and sick all over.

Shot. He still couldn't believe Beech was that crazy. But according to a quaking, sobbing Daisy, her father had shot Emily.

The amount of blood that flowed out of Emily's upper leg scared him senseless. Lots of blood. Too much blood.

Now, she was inside the Calypso Hospital emergency room, and Levi was out here in the waiting area, struggling to hold onto his sanity until he knew if she would be all right. Daisy sat in a padded vinyl chair quietly playing with Mason, though she was still milk pale and looked ready to cry at the drop of a hat. Levi could no more sit than he could fly. He paced up and down, back and forth, nagging every person in scrubs for information.

Before the ambulance arrived at the ranch, Emily had

regained consciousness briefly and opened her eyes. They were glazed as if she didn't know where she was. Blood loss would do that to you.

Levi had blurted, "I love you," like some kind of maniac, and when the corners of her mouth lifted the slightest bit, he said it again about a hundred times. She didn't smile anymore, but she'd let him know she heard.

Chanting the words in between prayers, he'd held her hand until the paramedic had pried his fingers loose and refused to let him, Daisy, and Mason ride together in the ambulance. So he'd driven his truck. Driven like Dale Earnhardt while praying as if he had a direct line to the throne room of heaven. Pleading for Emily to be all right so he could make up for all the stupid things he'd said and done. So he could tell her everything she needed to hear. He'd never prayed so much in his life.

At one point, he paused in his prayer-pacing to text the pastor. Marcus would pray. God would listen to a preacher.

I hear you, too.

Levi's eyes fell shut. *Thank you, God in Heaven. Emily needs you.* So did he, but God could work on him later. Emily first and foremost.

Fear not.

"Will she be all right?" He'd spoken aloud, but he didn't care if the whole world thought he was loony.

"Mr. Levi, Mason's real wet." Daisy looked toward him from a chair that swallowed her up, Mason propped on her lap. The usually happy girl's blue eyes weren't smiling today.

"The bag's in the truck." He glanced toward the door

to the parking lot. When was the last time Mason had been changed? He couldn't even remember. "I'll get it in a minute."

With her usual maturity, Daisy rose and handed him the baby. "I'll go, Mr. Levi. You wait for Miss Emily."

Her lips quivered. Tears sparkled on her pale lashes. Though tough as a bull hide, the little lady was as scared as he was. Levi put his free hand on her narrow shoulder.

In his kindest, most confident voice, he assured her, "You did good, Daisy. You saved her. God is in there with Miss Emily. She'll be all right."

"I prayed real hard."

"I know you did. And God heard. After I change Mason, I'll buy you a Coke, okay?" As if a soda would wash away the trauma of what she'd seen and experienced today. It wouldn't. Trauma that cruel never left. But a can of pop was the only thing he knew to do.

Daisy nodded and headed out to the truck, head down, steps unusually slow.

She carried too heavy a burden for such small shoulders.

He hadn't questioned her about what happened. She was too upset, and so was he. The sheriff would do that, but she'd said enough for Levi to know she'd been there. Poor kid. To know that. To have witnessed that.

If he wasn't so worried about the love of his life, he'd drive out to Beech's and do some bodily injury. The Caldwell brothers were on their way with Connie and Gilbert and probably half the town. They wouldn't be happy with Beech either.

Daisy returned, and Levi kept his word. After

changing the baby, he bought her a soft drink and tried to make himself sit down.

The Caldwells arrived, a barrage of worried faces. Connie came straight to him and gave him a hug. The knot in his gut loosened. Before he could guide the family away from Daisy's hearing and reveal all he knew, the emergency room door scraped open.

Every person in the room surged forward.

A nurse stepped out and gazed around at the crowd. "Levi?"

He stepped up. "Yes, ma'am."

"Emily's asking for the cowboy with the baby and the terrified expression."

That would be him.

Ace, Emily's oldest brother, pushed to the front. "She's okay?"

"She will be." The nurse moved to one side and held the door. "She said to tell the rest of you to sit down and relax and not to hurt anyone."

Nate snorted. "Smart aleck sister."

As worried as they were, knowing she hadn't lost her sense of humor lifted their spirits.

"Go, Levi." Connie took Mason from his arms. "She wants you."

She wanted him. *Him*. After all he'd done to hurt her.

A love so big he could hardly carry it pushed him through the door and into the emergency room. At the counter running along one wall, a nurse in blue scrubs tapped on a computer tablet. Above her, two metal cabinet doors hung open, displaying rows of medical supplies inside. An assortment of mysterious equipment lined the other walls. A sink, an oxygen set up, a beeping heart monitor. The fact that the heart beeping was Emily's scared him to death.

His gaze zeroed in on her. Covered to her chest with a white sheet, she lay on a table in the center of the room, tubes running into both arms. One dripped blood, the other some kind of clear liquid. A pronged tube hissed oxygen into her nose.

"Hey," he said, barely able to breathe and scared to touch her.

The hand with the clear liquid reached for him. "I'm okay."

He clasped her fingers in his. She was cold. "Do you need a blanket?"

As if waiting for someone to ask, a nurse placed a white blanket over her.

"Oh, that's warm." Her words were breathy as if she were exhausted. "Tell Daisy this is not her fault. She did everything right."

Levi nodded, throat clogged with emotion. Emily, thinking of others when she was the one injured.

"I have, but I'll tell her again."

"Stop worrying. Doc says I'll be fine."

A doctor in black-rimmed glasses, scrubbing his hands at the corner sink, glanced up and met Levi's questioning stare. He was young, not Doc Bridges, the physician Levi had known as a kid.

"She will be," the doc replied to the questions Levi wanted to ask. "We got the bleeding stopped, and after we get that bullet out and some antibiotics in, she'll mend quickly."

"Don't let my brothers do anything crazy." She squeezed Levi's fingers. "You either. Let the sheriff handle Beech. Promise?"

Right now, he'd promise her a trip to Mars if she asked. And he'd figure out a way to make it happen. "Promise. Now, stop worrying and let the doc get you fixed up."

The doctor, blue towel in hand, stepped close to the table. "Time for X-ray, Emily, and then on to the O.R. to get that bullet out. Your friend will have to leave now."

Levi leaned down and kissed her softly.

Her eyes filled with tears. After all she'd been through, it was his kiss that made her cry.

"Will you be here when I get out?" she whispered.

The question stabbed him through the conscience. "I'm not going anywhere, Emily. Now or ever."

A puzzled wrinkle appeared in her forehead. "Never? What about Texas?"

"I've tried living without my heart for fourteen years. Now, that I found it, I'd be a fool to leave it again."

Her eyes dropped closed, and a tear trickled down her cheek. Levi kissed it away and whispered, "You're my heart, Emily. I love you. Forgive me."

She just smiled.

EMILY WOKE to the sound of voices. Her brain was foggy, her eyes too heavy to open. Her mouth tasted like a combination of wet cotton and insecticide. She tried licking her lips, but they felt sticky as if someone had smeared them with a glue stick.

What in the world had happened to her? Where was she? Dreaming?

Yes, dreaming. She'd had a terrible nightmare. Someone with a gun. Searing pain. Blood. So much blood.

"She's coming around," a voice said. Nate, she thought. Her brother was here.

She heard boots shuffle against the floor, a door open, a voice she didn't recognize. "She was a lucky woman. The bullet missed the bone and only nicked the femoral artery."

"Artery? Was that why there was so much blood?" Ace's voice, worried, shaky.

The dream had been real. She'd been shot by Arlo Beech.

Levi had come for her. Levi had promised...something. She tried to pry her eyelids upward. They wouldn't cooperate.

Was Levi here? Had she dreamed it, or had he promised to stay with her?

A hand touched her cheek. "Hey, beautiful. Time to open those pretty green eyes."

Levi.

She sighed softly, relaxed, and drifted back into darkness.

When she woke again, her eyelids popped open. The lights had been dimmed. She looked around the space. She was in a hospital room. Outside was dark. Around her bed, three brawny cowboys sprawled in chairs or against the wall. Her brothers and Levi.

"Where's Connie?" And Daisy and Mason? Her throat hurt too much to say all their names.

Levi bounded up from his chair. Nate and Ace bolted upright as if her voice were an alarm clock.

"What did you say, darlin'?" Levi leaned over her. His red-rimmed eyes said he hadn't slept, and his whiskery jaw said he hadn't shaved.

She moved her thick tongue. "Connie?"

"She took Daisy and Mason to the Triple C for the night."

Emily wiggled her hand from beneath the sheet.

Levi latched on as if she were a lifeline.

"You stayed."

"Not leaving either."

"Good." She swallowed. "Can I have water?"

Levi fumbled with the pitcher before putting a straw to her lips.

"My throat's so sore."

"The surgery," Ace said. "They stick a tube down your throat."

Emily grimaced. Nate punched his brother's arm. "Don't be so graphic. She's been through a lot."

Levi stroked the hair away from her face. "Are you hurting? Do you need anything for pain?"

His touch was soothing enough. "No." She was still too groggy. "How's my leg?"

"Leg's good. Bullet's out, no permanent damage. Doc says you'll be immobile for a few days and really sore, but he expects a full recovery."

She nodded. "God was with me. He saved me."

"I wish He'd deflected that bullet for you."

"I think He did. The rifle was pointed at my chest. I ran." Big green eyes nearly did him in. "All I could think of was getting to you where I'd be safe."

"I always want you to feel safe with me, Emily." He kissed her forehead. "I'll protect you, take care of you, and I promise never to let you down again."

Nate cleared his throat. "Do you two need a little alone time?"

Ace grinned and whacked his brother with his hat. "Come on, Nate. Let the two love birds work this out before we have to shoot Levi, too."

"That's not funny."

"It sure as heck ain't."

The door opened, and two of her favorite cowboys took their leave.

Her other favorite cowboy eased a hip onto the edge of her bed, slowly, carefully, as if he were afraid she'd break. He still held her hand, and from the look of terrified determination on his wonderful, exhausted face, he wasn't going to let go any time soon. "I'm sure glad they left, 'cause I need to say something, and you know how hard that is for me."

She knew. Oh, how she knew. "You can tell me anything."

"Yeah, well, how's this for starters. I love you. I never said it to anyone in my life but you. Well, Mason recently. He's the one who made me realize how much words matter. When I was growing up, no one ever said those things to me. I didn't want him lacking in the love bucket."

She giggled. "The love bucket?"

"Told you I'm not good at this stuff." He looked to the side, hissed through his teeth and tried again. "All these years of running, roaming, I was looking for home." His gaze came back to her. "I was looking for you. I can't live without you, Em. I've tried. I hated it."

"Me, too."

"Stupid for me to move to Texas if you're here."

"It sure is. But you have a sign up at the ranch."

"I'll take it down as soon as I get home."

"Home?" The admission made her heart leap. Had he finally settled his feelings toward his family ranch?

"Yeah. Scott made that ranch a home. He left it to me and Mason. We belong there."

"What about your dad?" Slim Donley was a cancer he had to treat before he could ever be happy at the Donley Ranch.

Levi's eyes dropped shut. "I did a lot of praying today. God told me to let go of my old man. To let all of it go."

"Can you do that?"

"With the Lord's help, a man can do about anything. That's what Aunt Ruby told me."

"Ruby's a wise woman. You should listen to her."

"What my dad did...I can't change it. For so long, I thought you'd hate me because of him. I thought you'd see me as a reminder."

"It was never your guilt to bear, Levi."

"Getting that through my thick head has taken a long time, but I understand now." He lifted her hand to his lips and kissed her fingers. "I'm still so sorry about what happened that day, and if my dad was here right now, I can't say there wouldn't be trouble. Forgiveness takes time."

Emily asked the question that had haunted her for fourteen years. "Why did you leave without so much as a call?"

"More stupid on my part. My dad threatened me with prison if I didn't. I believed him."

Hers eyes widened. "He was the one who locked me in that stall, who attacked me. You did nothing wrong. He couldn't send you to prison."

"You were so upset. I didn't know how to comfort you. I didn't know what to say. All I could think of was making the old man sorry he'd ever touched you."

In retrospect, she should have reported the attack to the police, but Slim hadn't done the unthinkable, and she wasn't sure he would have. She'd been embarrassed, too. Even now, she couldn't stand the thought of anyone knowing what happened.

Mostly, Slim Donley had intended to humiliate her and embarrass Levi. "He never wanted you to date me," she said. "He was trying to break us up."

And he'd succeeded.

"Not because of you. My dad hated for me to be happy, and even more, he hated the idea that I would spend time with you instead of working like a slave on his ranch. He said you were too good for me." Levi stroked her hand. "He was right. You are."

Levi had stormed into the barn, yelling and swinging. She'd been crying so hard, she couldn't think or speak as he'd dragged her to his truck. All she'd wanted was to go home. She'd been a hysterical teenager. So had Levi.

The short drive from his ranch to hers had seemed interminable. He'd gripped the steering wheel with white-knuckled grimness and spoken not a word. She'd thought he blamed her. Now, she knew he'd been humiliated and ashamed of being his father's son.

All the way to the Triple C, she'd bent double, face in her hands, sobbing. Later, she'd told Connie she and Levi had had a fight. Even now, the lie bothered her. It was the only one she'd ever told to her surrogate mother.

"What happened after you took me home? I still don't understand. How could he threaten you with jail?"

He was finally talking, and she would not let him stop until he got it all out. The wound had festered long enough.

Levi's lips twisted bitterly. "I tried to kill him."

"Levi! No."

"I hated him, Em. We fought like tigers. I was younger and stronger, but he was meaner. I busted his face up pretty good, broke his nose, maybe a few ribs, but he got to his shotgun." A line of sweat appeared on Levi's forehead. The retelling was cathartic but painful too. "He told me to get off his property and never come back or he'd see me in prison. He had the damage from my fists to prove I'd attacked him. I believed him."

"I wish you'd told me. All these years of thinking I'd done something wrong, that you blamed me."

"What? No! Never." His shocked expression shifted to tenderness as he leaned close and stroked her hair. "Emily, you're the purest, finest person I've ever known. If my old man had called the police, everything that happened would have come out. Gossips don't always get the facts straight, and the facts were bad enough. I couldn't let you go through that. Gossip, stares, questions. Someone would have blamed you. You know how people are. I couldn't let that happen. You were embarrassed too much as it was."

Something sweet, tinged with bitter, twisted in Emily's chest. He'd loved her that much. "You were trying to protect me."

"Some job I did of that. My leaving only caused you more grief." He fell silent, pensive.

Emily raised a hand, tubes dangling, and touched his cheek. "The past is gone. This is the present. Let's live here."

"Em. Oh, Em. When I saw you lying in that field, I was afraid I'd lost you forever, and my whole world caved in. I regretted everything." He tipped his forehead against hers. "Back then, I was a kid without any sense. Don't let me be that crazy again."

"What about the manager's job in Texas?"

"I called Jack Parnell while you were in surgery."

Her heart jumped, and it had nothing to do with her medical situation. "You're really staying in Calypso, on the Donley Ranch—*your* ranch?"

A smile lit his eyes. "On one condition."

Fatigue began creeping up on her again. Her eyelids drifted down. "What's that?"

"You live there with me. With us, me and Mason. He needs a good mama to love him."

The drugs tugged at her consciousness, pulling her back into the shadows. "Mmm, sounds good."

"Will you marry me, Em? Will you be my wife?"

Her eyelids shot up. "What did you say?"

"This is probably the lousiest timing ever, and I don't have any fancy words, but marry me, Emily. Let me live in the same house with my heart. Let me be the man I always should have been for you."

To Emily, the timing couldn't have been better nor the words any fancier. "Soon?"

"The sooner, the better. I love you, I love you, I love you." He kissed her eyelids, her mouth, her cheeks, and her eyelids again.

His warm kisses felt so good, so relaxing. Levi was here. He would stay. She would be his wife, and Mason would be their son.

Her reply came in a drowsy whisper. "Love...you."

Then with a smile on her face, Emily drifted off to sleep.

EPILOGUE

L evi fidgeted like a man facing the firing squad. His about-to-become brothers-in-law, looking fancy in black hats and suits, circled around him like anxious coyotes ready to attack at the first sign of trouble.

Outside, car doors slammed, and voices filtered to him from the church foyer. He could smell the flowers. Or maybe that was his boutonniere, the palest pink rose he'd ever seen. It smelled pretty good, too. He drew in a big sniff, so excited, he hardly knew himself.

He was in a Sunday School room with Nate and Ace waiting for the signal to move into place down in front of the sanctuary next to the preacher. Emily was somewhere in the building, getting even more beautiful, if that were possible. He couldn't wait to see her.

After the awful scare with Beech, he could hardly bear to have her out of his sight. Six months, and he still woke in a cold sweat. But his Emily was a strong, independent woman. So strong, she'd convinced the Tompkinses that Levi was the perfect father for Mason, and the couple had dropped their custody suit. He'd been so relieved about the turn of events, he'd offered to keep in touch.

"Your tie's crooked." Nate grabbed for Levi's throat, and the groom-to-be tried not to flinch. Even though the brothers declared their pleasure that Levi had finally come to his senses, Emily was still their baby sister, their pride and joy, and these two bruiser cowboys would knock his head if anything upset her.

No way Levi would do that.

Ace drifted close to his brother and looked Levi up and down. He checked out the silver vest, the black tux, his brand new shiny black boots. "You're an ugly cuss. Don't know why she wants you, but she does."

Levi grinned. The nicest compliment a cowboy could pay another was to tell him how ugly he was. That and criticize his riding ability. Both meant he was doing something right.

"I'm a blessed man," Levi said.

"Yeah, you are," Ace growled. He'd always been the wild man of the Caldwells. Today he looked particularly feral. "Better treat her right or you'll answer to me."

"I aim to." He'd spend the rest of his life loving her, treasuring her, and making up for lost time. "If I ever even think about getting out of line, I fully expect you to knock some sense into me."

Ace clapped him on the back. "Won't be a problem."

"Hey." Nate lost his grip on the contrary tie and shot

his brother a cranky look. "I'm fixing a tie here. Beat on him later."

Ace grinned. Like a Doberman. "My pleasure."

Levi laughed out loud. He loved these guys. Though he missed Scott with a grief that would never end, he was proud to call these two cowboys brothers.

"Seriously, boys." He wished he knew how to express all that was in his heart for Emily. "You got no worries. Emily is the best thing that ever happened to me, and I'm finally smart enough to know it."

"Smart?" Nate dropped the tie again and pulled a face. "I wouldn't go that far."

The three men chortled, good-natured, happy to see this day arrive. Today was Levi's wedding to Emily, the woman who could have any man she wanted. But she'd chosen him.

Forgiveness brings good things.

You were right, Lord. Imagine that.

Aunt Ruby would be proud to know that God talked and that Levi listened and talked back. Either that, or she'd think he was nuttier than a squirrel tree. She was here. He'd have to ask her.

Forgiveness was a good thing. If he'd known how free he'd feel after letting go of his father, he'd have done it long ago. The incident that had defined him for years seemed small now. Distant. He credited the Lord and Emily with the change.

"Aren't you done yet?" With Nate's thick fingers between the tie and Levi's skin, Levi's throat was closing off.

The pressure released. "All done." Nate patted Levi's chest. "You look fairly decent."

"Good enough to marry Emily?"

"Not even close."

They grinned at each other, and Levi felt the weight of aloneness drifting away. The Triple C had sprawled across the Oklahoma landscape for decades. These men had roots and family. Now, he and Mason, too, would plant themselves on soil he'd once wanted to abandon with the woman who'd helped him find his way when he'd been lost.

He swallowed thick emotion, wanting to tell Nate and Ace how much their friendship, their acceptance meant. "Nate. Ace. I gotta say something."

Ace squinted at him. "If you run now, I'll break your kneecaps."

He'd just got those kneecaps fixed.

"He's joking, Levi."

"I know it."

"No, I'm not," Ace said.

Levi shook his head, loving the banter. "What I'm trying to say is, thanks. I miss Scott. I wish he was here more than I can ever express, but having you two to stand up with me today...well, it means a lot."

Two pairs of eyes held his, serious now. Levi struggled not to get crazy and spring a leaky face. As it was, his chest was about to explode. He was that emotional.

He was saved from disaster and a lifetime of cowboy teasing when Ace's cell phone mooed. He was the only man Levi knew who had a cow ringtone.

Ace glanced at the screen, shot them a weird look,

and stepped into the corner to answer his call. Nate and Levi exchanged glances and talked quietly while Ace finished his conversation.

When Ace slid the cell phone inside his jacket, his face had paled, a real task for a man with a permanent outdoor tan.

"What's up?" Nate asked.

"Step nine. The big one."

Levi had no idea what he was talking about, so he kept his mouth shut and listened. Anxious to get the wedding started, he was glad for the distraction.

"You found her?" Nate leaned close to his brother, voice low. "You found Marisa?"

"Took a private investigator. Same one you hired last year to track down Whitney's rotten cousin."

"He's a good man. Where is Marisa now?"

"I told the PI I was at a wedding, so we didn't talk much. He said he'd give me all the details tomorrow in his office." Ace sucked in a deep breath, clearly shaken. "He said I should prepare myself. Wonder what he meant by that?"

Nate's big rancher's hand squeezed the top of his brother's shoulder. "Don't know, but you're doing good, bro. After Marisa, how many more on your list?"

"Way too many."

"Part of the process, man. You'll get there. I'm proud of you."

The odd conversation swirled around Levi's head. Ace had found someone he'd been looking for. Someone he should be prepared to see. And what was this step thing he was talking about? Was Ace in AA or something? He'd have to ask Emily.

But not today.

Someone tapped on the door.

"Yeah?" he called. "Come in."

The most beautiful woman in the world poked her head around the door edge. She wore a poufy white veil and a big smile. "I'm here. Let's get married."

Levi's heart soared right out of his chest. They'd both needed time to heal physically—his surgically repaired knees and her leg—but the biggest healing had taken place on the inside. Now they were ready for the rest of their lives.

Ignoring Nate and Ace, he reached out a hand, and she took it. "I love you. You're beautiful."

"Wait till you see the rest of me."

He laughed. Her brothers growled. She glared at all of them. "I meant my dress."

Levi didn't care about the dress. He didn't care about the ceremony. But he cared about the family and friends waiting outside in the sanctuary, and most of all, he cared about Emily. He'd do anything to make her happy.

"You'll be beautiful with it or without it."

Someone jabbed him in the back. Ace, he thought, because he heard him mutter, "Kneecaps."

Levi ignored him. Ace had threatened him pretty much every day for the last six months. But the cowboy and his brother had also done his chores and baled his hay while Levi's knees healed.

They'd come to an understanding of pure friendship and brotherhood. They all fiercely loved Emily.

"Where's Daisy?"

"She's lighting the candles now. She looks beautiful in the blue dress Connie and I picked out."

Connie, with her loving, nurturing heart, had embraced the little girl as foster daughter while her father served time in jail. As far as Emily and Levi were concerned, Beech could stay locked up, and Daisy could remain in their family forever.

"Mason?"

"Connie has him, of course. You know how he loves his *abuela*."

His grandmother. Mason would know the deep, lasting love of family in a way Levi never had. "Sounds like everyone is set then."

"Everyone but us."

"Still want to marry me?"

She hooked a finger beneath his too-tight tie. "Better believe it, cowboy."

Levi took her hand, pressed the fingers to his lips, and then leaned close for the real thing. Her lips.

"Time to go."

The moment he'd been waiting for had finally arrived. He kissed his bride again, aware that he could kiss her all he wanted for the rest of his life.

As she moved away from the door, he and his groomsmen headed to the front of the church while some guy played beautiful piano music and another guy fiddled.

Connie sat on the front pew with Gilbert at her side and Mason in her lap. The baby was dressed in a onsie tuxedo, handsome as his late daddy, and Levi's best man in Scott's stead.

Nate stopped and took the little man into his arms before moving into place between Levi and Ace. Mason saw his uncle, and he kicked his legs, his mouth opened in a wide smile. Levi's chest swelled with love. He could feel Scott here beside him, smiling too, both through his child and in spirit.

Levi crossed his hands in front the way Emily had instructed and the wedding march began. Though he tried his best to appear calm, his pulse easily hit one-fifty when Emily appeared at the top of the aisle.

She came toward him, the dream he'd been afraid to dream. Their eyes met, and her lips curved. Her face glowed, radiant, a word he'd never used in his life. Maybe he glowed a little too.

Today he would marry his best friend, the love of his life.

Thank you, Lord, he thought, heart bursting with love and gratitude.

And as Emily reached his side and took his hand, Mason laughed, and Levi was absolutely sure he felt God smile.

ABOUT THE AUTHOR

Winner of the RITA Award for excellence in inspirational fiction, Linda Goodnight has also won the Booksellers' Best, ACFW Book of the Year, and a Reviewers' Choice Award from Romantic Times Magazine. Linda is a New York Times bestselling author.

Linda has appeared on the Christian bestseller list and her romance novels have been translated into more than a dozen languages. Active in orphan ministry, this former nurse and teacher enjoys writing fiction that carries a message of hope and light in a sometimes dark world.

She and husband Gene live in Oklahoma with their daughters.

www.lindagoodnight.com

ALSO BY LINDA GOODNIGHT

Triple C Cowboys

Twins for the Cowboy

A Baby for the Cowboy

A Bride for the Cowboy

Honey Ridge

The Memory House

The Rain Sparrow

The Innkeeper's Sister

The Buchanons

Cowboy Under the Mistletoe

The Christmas Family

Lone Star Dad

Lone Star Bachelor

Whisper Falls

Rancher's Refuge

Baby in His Arms

Sugarplum Homecoming

The Lawman's Honor

Redemption River

Finding Her Way Home

The Wedding Garden

A Place to Belong

The Christmas Child

The Last Bridge Home

The Brothers' Bond

A Season for Grace

A Touch of Grace

The Heart of Grace

Made in the USA
San Bernardino, CA
01 October 2018